Stranger on the Fens

To Vi

Best wishes

Keith Broughton

Stranger on the Fens

Keith Broughton

ATHENA PRESS
LONDON

STRANGER ON THE FENS
Copyright © Keith Broughton 2009

All Rights Reserved

No part of this book may be reproduced in any form
by photocopying or by any electronic or mechanical means,
including information storage or retrieval systems,
without permission in writing from both the copyright
owner and the publisher of this book.

ISBN 978 1 84748 510 6

First published 2009 by
ATHENA PRESS
Queen's House, 2 Holly Road
Twickenham TW1 4EG
United Kingdom

Printed for Athena Press

Prologue

The once-beautiful snow was now compact, solid ice. A bitterly cold wind relentlessly drove the icy rain hard on to the already treacherous surface. Why would anybody choose to be out on such a dreadful day? And yet they were. Sad sullen figures, clothed in their seemingly endless worldly worries. That was the view that he had from his blissful, beautiful, tranquil world.

He was surrounded by evergreen trees, flowers, the likes of which he had never seen before, all bearing fruits and colours quite rare to the untrained eye. Waterfalls tripped and gently caressed the rocks before easing down the stream of life.

On the banks were all kinds of animals, happily going about their daily chores, and all living together in perfect harmony. He felt an enormous sense of belonging to this place, he had found his solace.

He could be alone if he wished, yet he was surrounded by warmth. Loving, caring people, faces he was sure that he once knew, but now seeming to have no identity, and no desire for one.

He cast a somewhat disillusioned eye back into the cold. He knew that he had to go back; it wasn't by choice, but some powerful force was pulling him back.

He yearned to stay there, in this paradise, but the acknowledging faces casting sympathetic glances in his direction foretold his fate.

Chapter One

The rain drove relentlessly down on the weary man. He vainly tried, in an instinctive reaction, to pull up his collar above his neck, only to discover that all he was wearing was a rain-soaked woolly jumper; his attempt to hoist his jumper higher was thwarted by gravity pulling the sodden garment back down. A brief glimpse behind him painted a slightly brighter picture. The barely visible sunset, masked by a grey sky, told him that the west was to his rear, meaning that he was heading due east. But that was all that he did know. Why was he out on the Fens on such a dreadful day? Wearing so little, he must have been in a hurry to leave whatever was in the west. He blinked uncontrollably as the rain drove even harder into his face; his eyes were stinging as the salty substance rolled down his weary forehead and into his eyes.

'Excuse me, sir,' a voice hollered from a short distance to his right, 'are you lost?'

'I don't know,' he replied, turning to see where the voice was coming from. He recognised the man as a policeman, but the uniform seemed very old and strange.

'What on earth are you doing out here on the Fens in these conditions? And why are you so unsuitably dressed?' the Constable asked. The man just shrugged. 'You had better come with me, sir,' he stated, whistling for his dog. 'Whatever it is that you are running away from can't warrant freezing to death.' He placed a caring but cautious arm around the man's shoulder, and guided him back towards the town.

'My name is Constable John Franklin. I am with the local constabulary; and you sir, what may I ask is your name?' the officer asked. The man only shrugged once more. 'Well, fortunate for you that I was out in these here marshes walking my dog. Who knows what would have happened to you otherwise?'

Together they walked back down the hill towards the police station. Constable Franklin talked constantly throughout the journey, but gained little knowledge from the stranger he was addressing.

He looked for fear in the man's eyes as they approached the station, which he thought would tell him if the man had committed a crime, but all he could see was a vacant confusion, even a look of astonishment.

'I found this gentleman out on the Fens,' Franklin explained to his duty sergeant. Sergeant Thomas was a rough, gravel-voiced Welshman, with years of violence etched deep in every line on his weathered face.

'Well, what's he done, Franklin? He looks rather strange to me, boy. Lock him up; I dare say we will find a body later.'

'With respect, sir,' Franklin exclaimed, 'I think that the man is lost, in body and in mind, sir. I fear that unless we call Dr Mayfield, then he will not see the night through.'

Sergeant Thomas stared deep into the man's eyes, and then with a reluctant glance at Constable Franklin he said, 'Very well then, go get Dr Mayfield and tell him we have another waif and stray for him.' Franklin knew that he had to act fast as the man was now drifting into unconsciousness.

'You run and get the Doctor, Franklin, and leave this blackguard to me; if he dares move in your absence, then I will club him to death,' Sergeant Thomas ordered.

Doctor Edmund Mayfield was a caring, portly gentleman described by his peers as being 'years ahead of his time'.

'What can I do for you, Constable Franklin, on such a dreadful evening?' Dr Mayfield asked, standing at the door. Franklin explained that he had been out walking his dog, and had found a man fumbling his way through the fierce rain, out on the Fens. He explained enough to arouse the interest of Dr Mayfield, who ordered Constable Franklin to hold the door ajar while he went to fetch his hat, coat and bag.

The Doctor's house, which doubled as a surgery, was only a short walk from the police station. Within moments they were at the scene, which pleased Franklin, as he was duly concerned about the stranger's welfare – especially as Sergeant Thomas was *looking after* him.

After a brief examination, Dr Mayfield told Franklin, 'This

man has a fever; I shall need your help to transfer him to my surgery, where I can treat him.'

'Is that wise, Doctor?' Sergeant Thomas asked. 'I mean look at his clothing, he looks like a convict to me. He could be dangerous.'

'He could also be dead in a few hours if I do not treat him, Sergeant,' Dr Mayfield stated. 'Anyway, in his condition he can't harm anyone.'

Franklin took hold of the man's legs and Dr Mayfield his torso, and together they carried him back into the rain, and the short distance to Dr Mayfield's surgery.

They struggled through the wide front door of the surgery and laid the man down on the leather sofa. Mayfield rang for his housekeeper, Maud Johnson, and the maid, young Emily Todd. Maud Johnson was a frighteningly old, straight-talking spinster, who took great pride in her job as housekeeper, and spared no one a lashing of her tongue if she disliked them. Deeply religious, she was the honest, no-nonsense person that Dr Mayfield trusted most. Emily Todd could not be more the opposite if she tried: young, beautiful and extremely shy, very hard working, but yet to gain the trust of the Doctor.

'Help me disrobe this man,' the Doctor ordered. 'And please, Miss Johnson, not a word of protest, just do as I ask.'

'You would not listen even if I did, sir,' Maud Johnson replied, anxious to get in her views, 'so I will do as you ask.' Together they stripped the man down to his underpants and covered him with a blanket, then Dr Mayfield looked about his surgery for the appropriate remedy.

He lifted the man's hand gently, and offered him a tonic. The man sipped the drink, then closed his eyes and went back to sleep. Dr Mayfield ordered Maud Johnson and Emily Todd to take it in turns to watch over the man. 'If there is any change, then I must know immediately, is that clear?' he asked.

'Yes, sir,' they replied, and went about their duties.

'If that will be all, Doctor, then I shall return to the station,' Franklin said. 'I don't like leaving Sally with Sergeant Thomas for too long.'

'Sally?' Dr Mayfield asked.

'My dog,' Franklin replied, tipping his hat as a goodbye to the Doctor. 'I will need to speak to you in the morning sir,' he said walking toward the front door, 'and I will need to ask him a few questions, as you understand.'

Dr Mayfield nodded, and closed the front door behind Constable Franklin.

Chapter Two

Dr Mayfield was woken from his slumber by a gentle tap on his bedroom door; he sat himself up in his bed and commanded whoever it was to enter. It was, as he expected, Maud Johnson. She stood at the opened door with a lantern in her hand.

'He is awake, sir,' she spoke. She was always so calm; had it been Emily Todd then she would have banged on the door, barged in and screamed with excitement. However, Miss Johnson was used to the Doctor bringing unfortunate people home.

'Has he uttered a word of any kind?' Mayfield asked.

'No, sir,' the housekeeper replied, 'but he has had a couple of accidents in the night. Miss Todd is cleaning him up as we speak, sir.' The Doctor reached for his dressing gown, and together they hurried to assist Emily Todd. The man was sitting up, with a blanket over him; he looked quite dazed, and wore an inquisitive look.

'Do you know where you are, son?' the Doctor asked his bewildered patient. The man just shook his head. 'Do you know who you are?' the Doctor continued, but again the man shook his head. He gazed around the room; he knew something was not right, but just what, he did not know. He was overwhelmed by a sense of fear, but he could not remember anything.

'Where am I?' the man asked. Emily Todd raised her head, and fixed her eyes, childlike on the man. Dr Mayfield noticed this and fixed Emily with a stern look.

'We shall maintain a professional manner at all times, Miss Todd,' he said firmly. 'Sorry, Mr...?' he asked, waiting for the man to fill in the blanks with his surname, but no reply came. The man once again just shrugged.

Dr Mayfield raised his hand up over his mouth and rubbed his unshaven face, shaking his head from side to side. 'I want to help you, but I can not if you persist in being obstructive,' Mayfield snapped.

'I don't know who I am or where I am, I just can't remember anything,' the man replied, obviously worried. The Doctor told Emily Todd to get the man a clean set of clothes and to wash his old ones.

'I am going to have a wash and a shave,' he stated, 'then we shall take breakfast at eight.' He left the room and Miss Todd followed with the man's dirty clothes.

Maud Johnson looked deep into the man's troubled eyes. 'You are trouble,' she said aggressively, 'and what is more I do not trust you. So hear this; you do one thing to harm the good Doctor, and you shall have me to answer to.' Her grubby finger was wagging, while pointing at the frightened man. He opened his mouth to speak, but the words failed him. So he did what he did best to date, and just shrugged unknowingly.

Chapter Three

After Maud Johnson's vicious dressing-down, the stranger lay back down to rest his troubled mind. Dr Mayfield asked Maud for his usual breakfast and ordered that she make some porridge for the stranger. 'With plenty of sugar,' he continued, 'our friend needs to build up his strength, to be rid of his fever.'

'Whatever you demand, sir,' Maud reluctantly replied.

Emily Todd returned to the stranger's room, with some clothes that she had cadged from Dr Mayfield's part-time butler, Albert Lowe. Luckily for the stranger, Albert was working that morning, one of the two mornings a week when he would help Dr Mayfield do his rounds. Albert was a very tall, skeletal man and looked much older than his forty-nine years. Emily knew that Albert's clothes would be far too big for the stranger, but nonetheless as the butler had been good enough to go back home to get them for him, she would make sure that the stranger wore them. Emily stared into the man's tranquil face as he slept.

'Sir,' she called: no reply. 'Sir,' she called again, this time a little louder, followed by a nervous cough. 'I've brought you some clean clothes.' The stranger opened his tired eyes, and stared into Emily's eyes knowingly.

'Jane,' he asked, 'it is you, isn't it, Jane? But why are you dressed like that?'

'No, sir,' Emily replied. 'My name is Emily not Jane; you must still be delirious, sir.'

'My God, what is happening to me, Jane?' the stranger asked. Emily looked nervous and stood up to leave the room. 'Please don't go, Jane,' he pleaded. 'Please don't leave me; what has happened? Where am I, and why are you calling yourself Emily?'

'Oh, sir, please stop this, you are frightening me,' Emily replied, standing well away from the stranger's bed. 'I've told you, sir, my name is Emily, Emily Todd.' The stranger's eyes filled with tears as he struggled to come to terms with his strange whereabouts.

'I am sorry,' he stated, 'please don't fear me, Jane, I mean Emily.' Emily looked at the stranger and approached him with Albert Lowe's clothes.

'You must put these on, sir, when you feel your strength has returned.' Emily could not quite come to terms with how knowingly and lovingly the stranger looked at her; but it did not scare her, because she had felt strange feelings for him from the first moment she saw him. 'Do you know your name, sir?' Emily asked.

'Chris,' he replied, 'Christopher John Price. But I don't know where I am or how I got here.'

'Well that's a start, my good fellow,' Dr Mayfield interrupted as he entered the room. 'Now, can you tell us where you are from and what you were doing on the Fens last night?'

Chris, at first, seemed confident in his reply. 'I live in East-church,' he said, then he looked bemused. 'I do not know what I was doing,' he stated sadly. 'I remember having a row with Jane, my girlfriend,' he continued looking directly at Emily. His gaze then dropped, and glancing back at Dr Mayfield he continued, 'I went out to look for her, then, well, I don't remember the rest.'

'You didn't harm the lady, did you, Christopher?' the Doctor asked quizzically.

'Good lord no,' Chris replied, 'I could never harm anyone; that much I do know.'

Dr Mayfield rubbed his hand across his face. 'I believe you, my good fellow,' he said, nodding his head. 'Let's just hope a body doesn't emerge, for all our sakes.'

Chris feigned tiredness to gain time to familiarise himself with his new surroundings; the room was very old-looking to say the least. Directly opposite his bed was a ceramic bowl full of cold water, and a towel to the immediate right of the bowl. The wallpaper was brown patterned, in fact everything looked brown or wooden. *This can not be in my time*, Chris thought to himself.

Maud entered the room with the newspaper in her hand, pointing to the fact that there was no mention of a Christopher Price, and that to date no bodies had been found on the Fens either. Dr Mayfield looked over at the tactless Maud, and gave her a look that told her that she should not be reading his paper. The raised eyebrows and flattened crease of his lips, followed by a slight nod of his head, conveyed the message.

The Doctor took his paper off Maud and passed it over to Christopher. 'Take a look,' he gestured, 'something in here may jog your memory.'

Chris obligingly took the paper from his host, with both Maud and Emily eagerly looking at him for any signs of recognition. He dutifully browsed the front page of the large newspaper, but the frown on his face and the downturn of his lips suggested he had seen nothing to answer any of his questions.

But then the Doctor and the two waiting maids suddenly saw a change in the man – the blood drained from his face, he looked pale and frightened, and raising his eyes from the paper he stared directly into the Doctor's eyes.

'What is it, sir?' Dr Mayfield asked anxiously. 'Tell me now what you have seen.'

Chris lowered his eyes once more to the paper, and focused on the date; as he almost passed out with fear. 7 January 1898. He had suddenly found himself one hundred and ten years in the past.

Chapter Four

'Are you all right, Mr Price?' Dr Mayfield asked, but Chris had slipped deep into his memory; he had thought that something was wrong when the Constable had found him on the Fens. He remembered how quaint the police station had appeared, and how old-fashioned the two officers had looked. Even the approach to Dr Mayfield's surgery had looked somehow odd, but as he had been slipping in and out of consciousness he had not thought any more of it.

He scrolled through the memories of that last evening of 6 January 2008; he remembered having a nasty row with Jane, and her walking out on him. He also could recollect driving out to find her. He remembered that whenever Jane was down she would drive out to the Fens and go for a long walk to clear her head, so that's where he'd headed. The rain was intense, beating hard against the car. He had got out of the car when he thought he saw Jane walking ahead, pulling his collar up over his head, and buttoning up his coat. The driving rain had bitten deep into his face, turning quickly to sleet and then snow. He had called out Jane's name, but the figure turned briefly to look then just carried on walking. Chris remembered how ghostlike the figure was, but still fearing it was his beloved Jane he walked on. He tried to run but it was so cold, and the wind so strong, that he found it easier to conserve his breath and walk quickly.

With the figure of the lady still in sight, Chris had carried on heading out deeper into the icy night. It was then that the figure disappeared; Chris shouted and kept on walking and looking. How could she just disappear, he thought, he felt he was only a few yards away, and then she just vanished. For several hours Chris refused to give up his search, fearing that something bad had happened to Jane.

It was then that he started to get disorientated. He was so cold, and the weather seemed to be getting even worse. It was his love of Jane, coupled with guilt over the row, which kept him out on the Fens, frantically searching.

Hypothermia was now Chris's worst enemy. He was becoming tired and confused, and for some reason, in his mind he thought how hot he was, and so, like most victims of hypothermia, he removed his coat and it was not long before his mind was telling him to stop and lie down to sleep. Nature's way of making the inevitable death more pleasant.

He remembered lying down and then having what he could recall as a very pleasant dream of being in a beautiful warm, friendly, loving place.

Something in the back of his mind was willing him to get up and keep searching, although he didn't want to; he was so deep into this dream that he was quite content to stay where he was, but this persistent niggling forced him to get up and walk. He had no coat, as he could not remember where he had left it. He had no strength, just an iron will to get up and look for Jane. It was then that the vision of the lady appeared again right in front of him. He felt sure it was Jane, only this time she seemed to be dressed rather differently.

He had no strength to call her name, his buckling legs just endeavoured to follow the woman. He vainly followed to wherever she was leading him. Then, just like before, she vanished. Panic now set deep into Chris's mind. He could feel his strength slipping away, bouts of dizziness frequently stopped him in his tracks, and on many occasions he almost passed out; it was just his will now keeping him alive.

He could feel himself staggering like a drunken man, as wind, rain and snow relentlessly slowed him down almost to a standstill. His mind was alerted back to a brief glimpse of reality by the sound of a barking dog, and then in the distance he saw the figure of Constable John Franklin. The rest was all vague, as by then he was almost delirious and unconscious.

'Chris,' the Doctor snapped again, this time raising him from his recollections and back to reality. 'Are you all right?' he continued.

'Oh no, sir,' Chris replied: 'and if I told you why, I doubt you would believe me.'

Chapter Five

Emily Todd looked deep into the stranger's troubled eyes; something rang quite strange in her mind, although she couldn't put her finger on what it was.

Emily's face shone with beauty; she was just twenty years old, blonde haired and wore the complexion of an English rose. She was of slight build, and although she was just a maid she possessed an air of elegance about her, far higher than her station.

'I will help him into Albert's clothes,' she nervously suggested, 'if that is OK with you, sir,' she added quickly, looking at Dr Mayfield. He gave his nod of approval and placed an arm around Maud Johnson's shoulder, gesturing her out of the room. He asked Maud to go for Constable Franklin, to tell him that they now knew the man's name, and to ask if he wished to question him further.

Chris was puzzled by Emily's insistence to help him dress. He could also see a look of recognition in her eyes.

'Jane, is it you?' he asked. Emily shook her beautiful head sympathetically.

'No, sir,' she replied, 'my name is Emily Todd as I told you earlier, although…' she paused.

'Go on,' Chris replied, 'please.'

'Well, sir,' she continued, 'last night when they brought you in, I was in bed fast asleep, and I swear in my dreams I was out on the Fens guiding you towards the Constable.' She continued to tell Chris that this was why she was looking at him so strangely. Her eyes never left Chris's face as she explained to him about her dream; now here she was, nervously staring into the eyes of this rugged man from the future.

Chris was six feet tall, well proportioned, and twenty-eight years of age. He wore a two-day stubble of a beard that seemed to enhance his handsome looks. He cast his mind back to seeing what he thought was Jane on the Fens before she disappeared, and then to seeing who he now assumed was Emily, who had led him to safety. But how could it have been, how could she have been there when she was fast asleep in bed? Her dreams of being out on the Fens did concern and puzzle Chris somewhat.

Emily dutifully helped Chris into Albert's clothes; to her amusement, they fitted better than she had thought. She then helped Chris to his feet. His legs were still weak after his bout of hypothermia, but he was determined to get up and go out to explore his new surroundings; he ambled along to the door.

'And where do you think you're going, my good fellow?' Constable Franklin asked, as he strode through Dr Mayfield's front door. Franklin and Chris chatted; Chris was as honest as he could be without telling him of the time difference.

'Will you be staying local for a while?' the Constable asked.

'Yes,' Chris replied, 'but as yet I don't know where.'

'Well, my good fellow,' the Constable continued, 'in the absence of a body we have nothing to charge you on, so for the meanwhile we will leave it there.' Chris nodded to the Constable, and then made his way outside. If he had had any doubts previously, what greeted him outside confirmed the date and time of which he was now a part. Emily had obtained Dr Mayfield's permission to escort Chris about town. It was a sensible precaution; one reason being that he was still unsteady on his feet, the other that they could keep a watchful eye on the man.

Together they slowly walked down the road. Chris was amazed by the hustle and bustle of the main road; his eyes focused on the horse-drawn carriages, clattering about the town seemingly oblivious to any form of road safety. The signs all seemed so old and Dickensian, which they were to Chris, but to Emily it was all so modern. A beautiful aroma of freshly baked bread filled the air as they walked past the bakery. The high street that Chris was used to was filled with banks, building societies, hairdressers, video shops and the like: in this time there were none of these, although they did pass an old barbershop, which caught Chris's eye.

The women walking about all seemed so elegant in their long, flowing dresses; most of them wore hats with petite brollies on their arms in case of inclement weather. Chris found it hard to take it all in.

All of these people are long dead, he thought to himself, suddenly feeling tired after his ordeal. He sat on a park bench with Emily.

'So, Christopher,' Emily asked, feeling rather daring in using his name for the first time, 'where are you from?'

Chris opened his mouth to speak, but held back. 'If I told you, Emily, you would never believe me,' he replied, and stretched out his hand and placed it over Emily's. She quickly pulled her hand back towards her.

'Oh, sir,' she shyly exclaimed, 'that was rather bold.'

'Well,' Chris replied, 'where I come from it is a friendly gesture and not deemed to be bold at all.' He extended his hand over to Emily and gently put her hand back into his. Emily smiled, and for the first time looked comfortable to be with Chris.

Chapter Six

Chris sat on the bench for a while, still lovingly holding Emily Todd's hand. His mind cast back to his beloved Jane, the row they had had, and how he was stuck in this place a hundred and ten years in the past.

He looked at the old shops on the busy street; meat hung from the butcher's window; next door the draper's seemed to be busy. Further down a queue had formed outside the bakery as shoppers waited, their baskets on their arms.

Well-attired men in suits, top hats and bow ties went in and out of the huge building that was the bank. Chris felt uneasy and was overcome by a sense of panic. He tried to find some kind of logic in what had happened to him, or indeed what was still happening. All sorts of ideas were flooding his already troubled mind; one thought was that if he wished hard enough, he may just return to 2008. He closed his weary eyes and wished as hard as he could; he cautiously opened one eye, followed by the next, only to find a beautiful and deliriously happy Emily, lovingly smiling at him, still clasping his hand.

He wanted so much to tell Emily about it all, but logic told him that he would probably scare her into thinking he was mad. He just had to keep his own counsel, and try to find the purpose of his being there.

Emily asked about Jane, and showed concern as to if she was all right. Chris smiled at her, 'I don't think I will ever see her again,' he mumbled, 'but I do hope to God that she is all right.' It was then that he looked deep into Emily's eyes; he placed his other hand over hers, saying nothing, but his eyes told him that there was no physical difference between Emily and Jane. It was so uncanny that the only difference was Emily's hairstyle: it was long, just past her shoulders, in fact exactly like Jane's before she'd had it bobbed. The only other difference, of course, being time.

The sky filled with dark clouds as the winter sun started to disappear. A chill filled the January air as it started to snow. Loathe as she was to let go of Chris's hand, Emily tugged at his and said, 'We had better be getting back.' As they rose to their feet they were greeted by the familiar growl of Sergeant Thomas; his huge figure loomed towards them. He pressed his chiselled face into Chris's.

'Well, boy, you have made a rather speedy recovery haven't you?' he growled. 'I think you and I need a chat.'

The Sergeant told Chris that he would allow him to escort Emily back to the Doctor's surgery, and then he would like a word with him at the police station. Chris nodded in agreement, and watched as the fearsome figure took his huge strides towards the station. Sergeant Thomas had an ungainly gait about him, which bought a smile to the face of Chris, temporarily taking his mind off his fate.

Chris dutifully escorted Emily back to Dr Mayfield's surgery. 'I'll see you later,' he softly assured her.

'Later?' she replied quizzically. 'Later when?'

Chris smiled again. 'It's a saying where I come from,' he told her, then walked the short walk to the station.

His mind flickered back to 2008, or forward – he couldn't quite figure which was correct. Back in 2008 he was a computer technician; no use for anything like that in this era, he thought. But he knew that Sergeant Thomas was going to grill him, so he decided to come up with a story that he was a policeman in London, that he had left the force to travel after the death of his father, and had just got lost along the way. He was in fact telling the Sergeant part of the truth; he had lost his father quite suddenly to a heart attack two years previously, in 2006. At just twenty-eight years of age Chris thought he could get away with his story, and if need be could quite easily be a policeman in that particular era.

Sergeant Thomas looked every bit as evil as he sounded, but seemed to buy Chris's story. He looked Chris up and down and uttered in his deep Welsh voice, 'Well, boy, if you are intent on staying around for a while, then tomorrow I will talk to the Mayor and see if we can enlist you onboard.'

Chris promptly thanked the Sergeant and made his way back to the Doctor's house. He could not seem to get Jane off his mind; he tried to console himself with the fact that she would be OK, and told himself that there was nothing he could do where he was now to affect what was happening in 2008. He had the added worry of having no money and nowhere to stay, all he had was a set of borrowed clothes, and they didn't even fit that well.

A thought struck him that his driving licence and money was in the pocket of his jeans that Maud had taken to wash. This thought in mind he hurried back to the Doctor's house.

Maud stood motionless with her hands on her hips having answered the door to Chris. 'You're back then are you?' she greeted him. 'And I'll tell you something else, Mr-I'm-lost,' she continued, 'keep your hands off young Emily: she is not twenty-one 'til July, so be warned.'

Good job for Chris that Dr Mayfield hurried to the door to greet him; he was anxious to speak to Chris, to find out if he could remember any more.

'Please do come in,' Dr Mayfield invited Chris, motioning him toward the open door of his study.

'Please be seated,' he said. 'My name is Edmund Mayfield, though few people call me by my first name: most people think my name is Doctor,' he chuckled. This broke the ice somewhat, and made Chris feel more relaxed. The Doctor sat fiddling with his grey beard, and tweaking his handlebar moustache. He was only forty-eight but looked quite older; he was not obese, but was rather portly and stout, and his distinct lack of height did nothing to disguise his frame. Feeling an overwhelming sense of trust towards the Doctor, Chris thought it wise to tell him where he was really from.

'You're probably not going to believe this,' he started, 'but, well here goes…'

He told the Doctor all about where he was from, not just the town at the other end of the Fens, but from the year 2008. He told Dr Mayfield everything that he knew, from the first man on the moon, to all of the monarchs he could recite. All about cars, trains, planes, radios, televisions, even computers.

He told of the two world wars, 'The first will start in just sixteen years' time,' he told the Doctor. 'Remember the date, 1914.'

The Doctor shook his head from side to side, and scratched his greying beard. 'We shall keep all this to ourselves,' he said at last. While his logic told him that he couldn't quite believe Chris, his instincts did lean towards believing what Chris was saying. He had listened to his ramblings and thought that Chris was either mad, a compulsive liar, an amazing visionary or simply a confused but honest man.

Fortunately for Chris, he settled on the latter.

Chapter Seven

Chris smiled to himself as Maud Johnson entered the room. 'I have brought your own clothes to you, sir,' she stated, 'so now you can return Albert's to him.'

But as she handed his clothes over to him, his smile turned to a look of amazement. 'These are not mine,' he said handing them back to Maud. 'I was wearing jeans and a jumper.'

'I know of nobody named Jean,' Maud replied sarcastically, 'and I can assure you these were the clothes the Constable found you in.'

Chris looked over at Dr Mayfield; he was nodding in agreement with Maud. *How can this be*, Chris thought to himself. He took the clothes, which comprised of a pair of dark brown sackcloth trousers, and a white shirt with no collar. He checked the pockets, but before he could say anything, Maud handed over a wallet, which she had removed from his pocket. Her stern face was a picture as the wrinkles of her frown turned to a smirk.

'All of your money is there,' she stated. 'I counted it all myself: seventeen pounds and thirteen shillings.' Dr Mayfield just shook his head. Although he trusted his employee implicitly, he also knew what a gossip and a nosey person she could be.

Chris took the wallet, which he did not recognise at all, and looked inside for his driving licence; he found nothing. He just could not understand why his clothes and wallet were different. Even worse, his driving licence had vanished: the only proof that he had of his identity and the time from which he came. On the upside, at least he had seventeen pounds and thirteen shillings, which made him quite well-off in those times.

Maud promptly left the room, feeling rather happy with herself that she had put her point across once more. Dr Mayfield smiled over at Chris. 'You're a very tired young man,' he quietly spoke, 'and still very weak from your fever,' he added. 'If you are from another time, you can't expect your personal belongings to pass through with you.'

Chris was still too shocked to say a word; he was beginning to disbelieve his own story himself. It all made him feel weak and tired. Dr Mayfield told him he would have a bed made up for him in one of the spare rooms. 'You rest here for a while,' he told Chris, 'and I'll get Miss Todd to show you to your room when it is ready.'

Chris, still feeling the after-effects of the shock, could not find the words to say anything so he just nodded to the Doctor and smiled. As he sat waiting, everything was racing through his troubled mind; he looked at his clothes and his wallet, and still could not recognise anything.

He was brought back to reality by a gentle tap on the door; it was Emily Todd, wearing a beautiful smile. 'I have come to show you to your room, sir,' she smiled. They left the study and headed for the grand spiral staircase. The Doctor's was a massive house, full of antiques, with many splendid rooms; huge paintings of family portraits and landscapes adorned the walls of the staircase and corridors. Emily tiptoed and put her finger to her mouth in a shushing motion as she passed Maud Johnson's room. Chris offered a tired smile, but still very bemused by the day's events, he had far too much on his mind for levity. Emily opened the door to Chris's room; the room itself seemed twice as big as the apartment in its entirety that he and Jane had shared back in 2008. There was a four-poster bed, a wash bowl and an armchair to the right of the bed. Thick, dark brown curtains, hung from the bedroom window, and over to the left of the window was a large writing desk, opposite the bed itself were two large double wardrobes, and to the left of them a full-length, free-standing mirror. Chris wondered to himself just how much a place like this would fetch in 2008.

'Will that be everything, sir?' Emily asked, deep down hoping that Chris would say no. 'No,' he replied much to her satisfaction. 'Please don't go; well, not just yet.' Emily smiled, and her beauty radiated round the room. Chris gestured her over toward him as he sat down on the armchair. He gently took hold of her hand, and clasped both of his hands over hers. 'I trust you, Emily,' he whispered. 'There is so much that I do not know, but need to find out,' he continued. 'I don't know what I am doing here, or even how I got here, but I have come to the conclusion that I am here for a reason.'

Emily looked unsure of what Chris was saying, but she also knew that she felt safe and secure whenever she was close to Chris, and did not fear him, although her trusting nature could not prepare her for what was to follow. Chris calmly pulled Emily towards him, and gently kissed her on the lips; she had never been as close to any man before, and even shocked herself by her complete failure to refuse Chris's charms. Instead she found herself getting closer to Chris's warm embrace. Their bodies locked in a moment of passion, a moment that Emily wanted never to end. Chris pulled his lips away from Emily's, and held his outstretched hands on her shoulders.

'You're all I've got in this world,' Chris warmly told her. Emily was speechless, she just could not stop smiling at the man she was now falling in love with. Although Chris was being quite literal in what he said, he too had strong affections for Emily; in his own mind, it was Jane he was kissing: same person, same body, just a different time.

Chapter Eight

Chris watched Emily leave the room, and then promptly got out of old Albert's clothes. He hoisted himself on to the bed and lay there, trying desperately to unravel the day's events, and to try to make some sense or purpose out of it all. But his mind and body were far too tired and weak to think or do any more, and he fell into a deep sleep of pure exhaustion. His subconscious mind drifted in and out of lucid dreams. He saw himself lying unconscious in a hospital bed, Jane standing over him crying uncontrollably; he heard voices saying 'He is very weak, but he is fighting,' then he saw Jane bend over towards him. She kissed him tenderly on the lips and said, 'Keep fighting, Chris, please don't give in.'

'I'm OK!' he shouted back at Jane; 'I'm OK, please help me.'

He must have been shouting aloud because he woke with a start, to find Dr Mayfield and Emily standing over his bed. The Doctor, fearing that Chris's fever may be returning, ordered that Emily watch over his patient; she dutifully agreed, promising the Doctor that if he got any worse she would alert him immediately. Dr Mayfield left the room, and Emily sat in the armchair watching over Chris. He didn't like to tell Emily that it had just been a bad dream; in fact her presence there comforted him somewhat, and so he just smiled and drifted back off to sleep. Emily turned down the gas lamps and watched over her new love.

Chris slipped back into his dream. Again he saw himself lying unconscious in his hospital bed; his parents were now there comforting the quite inconsolable Jane.

'You do know that you may have to face the possibility of switching off his life-support machine, don't you?' the Doctor quietly whispered to Jane and Chris's parents.

'Jesus no,' Chris shouted from his slumber. 'No, no, no.' Again he woke with a start to find Emily mopping the beads of sweat from his brow. 'It's OK, my love,' she whispered, 'I'm here.'

'Oh dear God, Emily,' Chris cried out. 'What is happening to me?'

He sat up in bed, drinking water from a glass that Emily had handed him. He regained his composure, and offered a weak smile to Emily. He held his arms outstretched, and with his hands motioned Emily toward him. He held her so tight to his breast that he could feel her heart racing.

'I feel like I have known you for a long time,' she whispered into Chris's ear.

'Oh believe me, Emily, I have known you a lifetime,' Chris replied. Although confused by his retort, his words comforted her nevertheless.

The embrace was followed by a lingering kiss; Chris heard Emily moan gently as he cupped his hands over her breasts, then kissed each one tenderly. He pulled her over so she was lying beside him on the bed and pulled off her nightgown over her head, exposing her beautiful young naked body. Despite still feeling tired, Chris was aroused by an overwhelming sense of passion: he made love to Emily.

They lay naked next to each other, still in a warm embrace, as Chris said, 'That was the most beautiful thing ever.' Emily just smiled and nestled closer to Chris, and they both fell asleep. He woke a couple of times in the night, and hugged Emily closer to him; her fresh smell of purity would stay with him 'til the day he died. He gently stroked her hair, and fell back to sleep. He dreamt a few more times the same dream, but each time a slightly different scenario. Either Jane was by his side, holding and kissing his hand, or his parents were there too, each time telling him to hold on and not give up the fight.

Chris was brought back to reality by a sharp tap on the door, followed immediately by the entrance of Maud Johnson. Chris panicked; he feared the worst straight away, and turned to where Emily was lying. To his astonishment and immense relief she wasn't there; a quick glance toward the armchair showed him where she was. He looked quizzically over at Emily: had he dreamt that as well, he pondered.

But the look of happiness and contentment on her beautiful face told him that *that*, at least, was reality.

Fortunately for both of them, Maud did not suspect a thing. 'I will take over from here,' she told Emily. 'You try and grab a couple of hours' sleep,' she continued, handing Chris a strong cup of tea.

Chris thanked Maud effusively, and drank his tea before falling deep into a dream-filled sleep. What seemed like only seconds later, but proved to be hours, Chris was woken by Dr Mayfield. He excused Maud of her duties, and after informing Chris that it was well after midday, he decided to give him a check-up.

'Your temperature seems to have receded,' he informed Chris. 'Think you could be on the mend, young man,' he told him, 'although you are not safe yet.' Chris sat up in bed and told the Doctor of his dreams, explaining that it all was – or at least seemed – so real. Dr Mayfield pulled his chair closer to Chris's bed. He looked Chris directly in the eye and quietly said, 'I've taken you in on trust, Christopher; now you are to trust me. For what I am about to tell you is in strict confidence between only you and I.' Chris gave his word of honour to the Doctor and listened intently to what Mayfield told him.

Dr Mayfield informed Chris that, as well as being a doctor, he also performed hypnosis. He had tried to cure patients of their ills via this method. To most of his peers, Dr Mayfield was years ahead of his time in not being frightened to try out so-called quack remedies. To the general public, he tried to keep a low profile on his less conventional methods, fearing being labelled a fraud. He went on to tell Chris that during these hypnotic trances many of his patients actually regressed to previous existences. Although he knew that regression could not help Chris because he was, or at least thought he was, from the future, nonetheless, the Doctor believed that if Chris was agreeable to the trial of hypnosis, it may help him in his quest for answers.

Chris listened to what the zealous Doctor was telling him and, nodding his head, agreed to try to be hypnotised. 'When do we start?' Chris enthused.

'Right after you have washed and shaved,' the Doctor smiled, handing over a cut-throat razor to Chris. Chris looked at the razor, and was filled with panic as he watched the Doctor leave the room. *How the hell am I going to use this*, he thought.

Maud entered the room with a jug of hot water, which she brusquely put into the wash bowl. Chris looked rather helplessly at the nagging spinster, and it must have worked because she took the razor off him. 'No point in trying to play the brave man when you're obviously still too weak to do things for yourself, boy,' she snapped, taking the shaving brush in her hand and lathering up Chris's face. In reality Chris was almost as nervous letting her shave him as he was in trying to perform the deed himself; but as he had never even held a cut-throat razor before today, let alone shaved with one, he felt marginally more at ease in letting Maud perform the task.

Chapter Nine

Fresh, awake, clean-shaven without a single cut on his face, and now dressed in what he was told were his own clothes, Chris hurried swiftly and anxiously to Dr Mayfield's study.

Dr Mayfield sat Chris down in a wide armchair and told him to relax. He had no charm or watch on a chain swinging from side to side; instead he just used his calm, quiet and relaxing voice to slowly put Chris into a hypnotic trance. He gave his instructions to Chris, and slowly and deliberately started counting to ten. Whether it was Chris's recent trauma or his willingness to go under, either way, before the Doctor had reached ten Chris was under his spell.

'Where are you, Chris; what do you see?' the Doctor asked. Chris told him that he was in a hospital room, consisting of only one bed, and that he was standing over himself, looking down at his body, which was wired up to a life-support machine. He went on to say that his girlfriend, Jane, was sitting by his bedside; her eyes were all red and swollen from the endless tears that she had shed for her love.

'What is the date and the exact time, Chris?' the Doctor asked.

Chris scoured the room to find a clock on the wall. 'It is 1.15 p.m. on 8 January 2008,' he replied.

Content with Chris's answers, Dr Mayfield took notes and then continued his questioning. He instructed Chris to go back two days, to what happened on the night he took to the Fens. Chris went on to tell the Doctor that he knew that Jane would be going for a walk on the Fens, as she always did when she was down or wanted to clear her head. He explained that he drove his car to where he thought Jane would be. He got out of his car and walked; the weather was abysmal – heavy rain, sleet, and later snow. He told the Doctor how he thought he saw her in the distance; he called out and then hurried after her.

It was after he became confused and unwell that he lay down

to sleep, having shed his coat while coming down with hypothermia. He had felt himself in a strange but beautiful place; he described it to the Doctor as being beautiful, warm, surreal, filled with love and beautiful flowers, trees and plants of different colours, like he had never seen before. He felt a pulling force, fiercely tugging him back into the cold, rugged terrain that he knew as the Fens. He did not want to leave this place, but felt compelled to go back into the cold. It was on his return to the freezing-cold Fens that, although the weather was the same, everything else was different. He saw what he thought was Jane and stumbled aimlessly into her direction; it was just before he was about to collapse, with his last ounce of strength, that Constable Franklin discovered him. Prior to that, the apparition he had thought was Jane, but who he could now swear was Emily, had vanished.

Chris was sweating profusely, and the Doctor could see his patient was visibly shaken. Armed with enough evidence to believe Chris, and try to help him, the Doctor started counting down from ten. 'Five, four, you're waking up, Chris, three, you're safe and sound and almost fully awake, two, one.'

'Welcome back, Chris,' the Doctor quietly spoke. 'Whatever you have gone through is far beyond my comprehension,' he added. 'I am quite unsure as to how I can help you, but I promise that I will try.' The Doctor was amazed at what Chris had told him; he was astonished yet interested in this 'life-support machine'. But what held his interest most of all was Chris's precision in the time and the date. He invited Chris to go and relax, in case he was overcome with tiredness, while he would ponder on what Chris had told him and how he could help him; that is, if he could help him at all. As Chris headed toward the door, Dr Mayfield called him back.

'Emily Todd,' he whispered, 'she's a gentle, lovely girl. She comes from a very troubled background.' He went on to explain that Emily's brother, Edward Todd, was a thief and a villain; her father had also been a notorious crook, before he died. He had felt sorry for Emily, who was left all alone at fourteen after the death of her father. With her brother in prison and her mother already dead, all that was left for her was the workhouse, or maybe even a dreaded life of crime, so he took Emily under his wing. 'I can see that she is very fond of you, Chris,' the Doctor said. 'Please take great care of her.'

Chris nodded toward the Doctor, and felt obliged to tell him about the uncanny yet exact resemblance between Jane and Emily.

'It's like it is the same person, only separated by time,' Chris explained.

Dr Mayfield scratched his greying beard. 'So,' he replied, 'the apparition you saw on the Fens, first in your time, and then in ours, was in fact Jane becoming Emily?'

'That's how it appears,' Chris replied to his confidant; 'strange, but true.' The Doctor again scratched his beard and shook his head from side to side; he waved his right hand in a motion for Chris to leave the room. Not another word passed between the two gentlemen as Chris walked toward the door; a mutual respect, even admiration now existed between the two and enough had been said on the matter already. It was now time to ponder the situation, and try to find a solution.

Chapter Ten

Feeling shattered after his hypnotic experience, Chris went back up to his room and had a lie down. He fell into a deep sleep, and almost immediately slipped back into his dream. He could see Jane and his parents standing over his bed; the clock on the wall said 2.15. He glanced down and looked at himself lying helpless on his hospital bed. The Doctor was there too, an Asian fellow, tall and dapper. 'Still no change,' he said to Jane in his accented English. He assured them that Chris was still fighting, and that he was having the best attention possible. It felt so strange to Chris looking down on himself, as if he was a different person.

Jane grasped Chris's hand and whispered, 'I love you, Chris, please don't give in, please.'

It was Chris's weeping that woke him up; rubbing his tear-stained eyes, he wondered which was the dream and which was reality. His sobbing was broken by Emily tiptoeing into his room. She quietly closed the door behind her and playfully leapt onto Chris's bed. The laughter and play soon turned to passion, and before they knew it they were once again locked in bodily passion, frantically making love. After exploring each other's bodies they lovingly lay next to each other, Chris stroking Emily's hair, while she just gazed deep into her lover's eyes.

Chris had only known Emily for a little under two days, yet the lovemaking had never felt more natural; it was like it was meant to be, and as though he had known Emily for years.

'I love you, Chris,' she whispered. 'Please don't give in, please.'

Chris lifted his head; those were the exact words that Jane had whispered to him in his dream: *how could this be*? he thought. His eyes locked on to Emily's. 'Why did you say that?' he asked.

'I'm sorry, Chris,' Emily replied. 'Should I not have been so bold as to declare my love?'

'Oh, no,' Chris replied, 'that was beautiful, honest,' he continued frantically, nodding his head. 'No, I meant why did you say "Don't give in?" '

'I do not know,' she answered. 'I would just hate for you to give in and go away,' she added. Chris smiled at Emily. He told her how sweet she was, and that even if he wanted to, at this moment in time he was going nowhere. He was in fact shocked by the words Emily had spoken; they were the exact words that Jane had spoken to him. Try as he could, he could not unravel the mystery that he was a part of. And what amazed him even more were the amazing parallels between the two lives.

Chris held Emily's hand tight. 'I am glad you said what you did,' he told her. Emily looked back at Chris. 'Well?' she added inquisitively. Chris smiled again at her beauty and pure innocence. 'I love you too, Emily,' he replied in long-awaited response. They embraced and lay together. Chris asked Emily about her past, and where she saw her future.

To his astonishment she had never made plans for a future. She explained to him that her past was so violent and troublesome that she was just glad to be alive, and took each day as it came; and that it was not until now that she thought she had a purpose in life. She went on to tell him that she was extremely proud of her honesty, considering the paths that she could have chosen in life. That is why she respected Dr Mayfield as much as she did. 'He is more like a father to me than my real father ever was,' she told Chris, with tears rolling down her rosy cheeks.

Chris listened intently, and held her hand as he took it all in. Their moment of intimacy was interrupted by a knock on Chris's bedroom door. Emily leapt out of bed and hid in the wardrobe; they both had to restrain themselves from chuckling like two naughty schoolchildren.

'Come in,' Chris shouted. Dr Mayfield entered the room, bursting with excitement. Chris sat rubbing his eyes, trying to convince the Doctor that he had been sleeping. The Doctor sat down in the armchair, as Chris sat up in bed.

'I think that you died,' he told Chris. 'That place you described, the one with all the lovely flowers, plants, and serene colours, well that was paradise, heaven, the other side: whatever you desire to call it,' he added. 'Then you came back: but you are actually reliving a past life.'

Chris could not take it in at all, although as far-fetched as it all seemed, it did make some sense to him.

He opened his mouth to speak but the words eluded him. He could only shake his head from side to side as he tried to take in what the Doctor had just said.

Chris looked over again at the excited Doctor. 'And the solution?' he asked.

The Doctor just frowned and shook his head as he rose to his feet. 'I haven't quite got that far,' he replied. 'Maybe we should both sleep on it tonight,' he added as he walked toward the door. As soon as the Doctor closed the door, Emily opened the door of the wardrobe and stepped out. Just as she got her foot out of the door. The Doctor re-entered the room, and quick as a flash Emily leapt back into the wardrobe. As serious as all of this was, Chris just couldn't help but laugh. Dr Mayfield looked pleasantly surprised by Chris's response, but what he had to say wiped the smile straight off his face. 'You are, as we speak, living parallel lives,' the Doctor stated. 'The only logical solution is that you have to die in one of them.' He then left the room, leaving Chris to contemplate his fate.

Chapter Eleven

It was a less jovial and a more sombre, even tearful, Emily that emerged from the wardrobe. She walked over to Chris's open arms and they embraced. 'I love you, Chris,' she whispered. 'Please do not give in, please.'

He assured Emily that while he had no idea what he was going through, or how he would deal with it, death was not an answer.

Chris kissed Emily tenderly on her lips; he gently wiped the tears away from her face as he bade her goodnight. Despite all that had happened to him, and all that was going on in his life, Chris still found it easy to sleep. Such was the exhaustion he was enduring.

It wasn't long before he slipped back into the same dream. Jane was still keeping a vigil by his bedside. But this time the mood looked even more sombre; his parents were doing their best to sooth the sobbing Jane.

'We are going to have to drain some of that fluid off his brain,' the Doctor told Jane and Chris's parents. Porters entered the room and proceeded to wheel Chris, on his bed, down towards the theatre. Jane walked alongside him, and went as far as she could before she saw him disappear through the theatre doors.

'Oh dear God,' she cried, 'please don't let him die.'

Chris felt himself being pulled back, and all went blurred.

He woke, quite early in the morning, with a very bad headache; so bad that he could barely open his eyes. So it was quite a relief for him when Dr Mayfield knocked on his door.

After being asked to enter by Chris, the Doctor asked how his patient was. Chris explained that he had a very bad headache, and asked the Doctor if he had anything for it. 'I will see to it for you,' he assured Chris; 'then, when you're well, we will talk further.' He rather disappointedly left the room; he had hoped to talk to Chris some more, and try to find out if he had had any more dreams.

Emily entered the room with a bowl of water and a towel; she lovingly placed the towel in the cold water, and gently placed it on Chris's forehead. Although in a lot of discomfort with his bad head, Chris still had to smile: he had hoped for some Ibuprofen or paracetamol at least. He must have forgotten where he was, or at least what era he was in.

He must have dozed off for several hours, but when he woke Emily was still patiently sitting by his side.

He stared into her beautiful blue eyes. 'Thank you,' he whispered, 'I do love you, Emily.'

He felt recovered from his headache and strong enough to make love to Emily. Each time they made love it just seemed to be pure and as though it was meant to be. After a long and passionate embrace they both got dressed; Emily returned to her duties, and Chris hurried downstairs to see Dr Mayfield.

'Come in,' the Doctor replied to Chris's tap on the door. He promptly entered the room and sat facing the anxious Doctor. 'Well?' the Doctor asked.

'Yes,' Chris replied. 'Yes, I have had the dream again.' He went on to explain how he saw himself, and how he apparently had fluid on his brain. He had no medical knowledge, so he didn't know if he was having cerebral bleeding or he had a blood clot. But even stranger, it now seemed that everything that was happening in 2008 was also occurring in 1898: the headache, the dizziness, Emily uttering the exact words that Jane was saying in 2008.

'Like I said, Christopher,' the Doctor chipped in, 'you are living on two different planes, and you are indeed living parallel lives.' He went on to explain to Chris that he thought when he had found his paradise maybe he was not meant to come back; maybe things all got muddled up in the process.

'But I was dragged back,' Chris snapped. 'I was happy in that place; trust me, I didn't want to come back.' They both sat there facing each other, speechless for a moment. Chris broke the tension by expressing his new fears. He explained that when he had had his headache, and he fell back asleep, he did not slip into the dream. 'Tell me,' Chris demanded. 'Does this mean that I have died in 2008?'

'There is only one way to find out Chris,' the Doctor replied. He looked over at Chris, and Chris just nodded: he knew what the Doctor meant

'Are you ready, Chris?' the Doctor asked. 'Then relax and we shall start.'

Dr Mayfield started counting up to ten, and Chris slipped deeper and deeper into a hypnotic trance.

Chapter Twelve

'Where are you, Christopher; what do you see?' the Doctor asked. Chris explained he could see Jane crying uncontrollably; his parents were desperately trying to console her. The hospital room was empty, and all Chris could hear was Jane repeating: 'Why, why, why?' she then pressed her head deep into Chris's mother's breast and sobbed some more.

He relayed this back to the Doctor, who although trying to maintain an optimistic stance did in fact fear the worst. 'How is your head, Christopher? Do you feel any pain?' the Doctor asked.

'I feel nothing,' Chris replied. 'I feel numb.'

Chris felt helpless. It seemed that he was only able to see himself in 2008 when Jane was with him; as was now, when they were separated, he could only see Jane. He heard his parents ask Jane if she had considered, donating his organs. She nodded and sobbed, 'Yes.'

Dr Mayfield could see Christopher visibly becoming agitated, so he decided to terminate this particular session and after counting down from ten to one, Chris awoke from his hypnosis. The Doctor was very interested in this mention of organ donation; it was something else that strengthened Chris's case in telling the Doctor he was from 2008. Not that Mayfield disbelieved him. Chris explained that it was now very popular for unfortunate relatives of recently deceased people to donate their organs, and that heart, liver and kidney transplants were very much everyday occurrences. Dr Mayfield was utterly amazed by what he had heard.

'And brains?' he asked. 'Has anybody performed a brain transplant to date?'

'No,' Chris smiled, 'not as yet.'

The two men sat staring at each other, Chris scratching his stubble, the Doctor tweaking his handlebar moustache. After a great deal of soul-searching and contemplating, Dr Mayfield broke the silence with the exact words that Chris did not want to hear.

'I think you are no more in 2008,' he stated.

Chris looked over at the solemn Doctor and said, 'You mean…?'

'Yes, Chris, you are dead; in 2008 you are dead.'

It made sense. Why else could he see only Jane and his parents; why did he feel no more pain; why were they preparing to donate his organs?

It was all too much for him to take in, and he broke down. He placed his weary head down into his hands and cried uncontrollably.

The Doctor, being of true Victorian stock, did not know how to deal with another man crying. He did what he thought was best and tried to comfort Chris with words, rather harsh ones at that.

'Now, now,' he said, 'you're still alive in 1898, take comfort from that, young man.'

To Chris it was no comfort, for he had lost his true love, Jane, and deep down he knew that he would never see her again, at least not in 2008 anyway. And here he was trapped in 1898 both in mind and body.

'Christopher,' the Doctor snapped, 'I do not know of the transplants and the likes of which you have described of your time, but I do know the general law of physics, and I do know that it would be physically impossible for you to walk back into your own body in 2008; because here you are a physical man, in shape and form: you are not a ghost, you actually exist.'

Chris knew what the Doctor said made perfect sense; it was just too hard and too much to take in at this present time.

He made his excuses and left the Doctor to ponder further. A long walk seemed the only answer to clear his mind, or at least to endeavour to bring himself to terms with what lay ahead.

This time he ventured out alone, unescorted, and not too bothered anyway. He wasn't too scared to just walk as far as he could; all of the town seemed so unfamiliar to him. He stared right through the people he passed in the cobbled streets, as if they were all ghosts, as in reality in 2008 they were, but he knew he had to try to forget 2008, as this place full of period-dressed people was now his only home and era.

Everything that he knew was in 2008; all his knowledge was acquired there. He knew how to drive, yet he didn't know how to control a horse-drawn carriage; he knew how to play CDs, DVDs, programme the TV, operate and even repair computers; none of that was of any use to him here.

He was stopped in his tracks by the welcome sight of the Bell Tavern. 'Good food and ale' the sign said on the board outside of the tavern. Feeling a thirst, and quite hungry, Chris decided to venture inside. *What do I have to lose?* he thought. In fact as he walked through the door of the smoke-filled room, he wasn't even sure how far he had walked; he remembered passing many people, yet he hadn't taken notice of any of the sights along the way: such was the state of his confused mind. He approached the bar with caution.

'Yes, sir; what will it be?' a busty and rather ill-dressed barmaid asked him. 'A pint of lager, please,' Chris replied, 'and what's on the menu?' he asked.

A very confused barmaid stared right through him as she asked, 'And what on earth is "lager" and "menu"?' Chris realised that he had been so busy trying to acclimatise himself to this place that he had forgotten what actually did and did not exist in 1898.

'I'll have what those other gentlemen have got,' he said, feeling more at ease, and deciding to play things safe.

'Right then, sir,' she replied. 'Ale and a pie it is then, and that will be tuppence farthing, please.' Chris dared not even ask as to what meat was in the pie, as he held out his hand helplessly, giving her a shilling, but not sure whether he had given her enough, or indeed whether he would receive any change.

'Don't look like you're from around these parts, sir,' a gravelled voice observed from Chris's immediate left. He turned to see a well-built, dishevelled man with his hand extended towards Chris. Chris shook the man's hand and mumbled that he wasn't from this particular town, but lived just the other side of the Fens.

'My name is Christopher,' he continued, 'Christopher Price.' Still shaking the hand of his new-found friend.

This man looked rough. Chris could see that he must be

roughly the same age as himself. He had teeth missing from his dishonest-looking smile, and seemed to be wearing more than enough battle scars deep on his face. He had an ill-fitting jacket, which had buttons missing, barely covering a dirty stained white shirt; he had no tie on, just a scarf, or cravat, which he had tied around his neck. His trousers, also, looked like they did not fit, as they were held up well above the waist, by the thickest looking leather belt that Chris had ever seen on a man.

'You can call me Ed,' the man replied, letting go of Chris's hand and still grinning wildly, 'but to the local Beak,' he continued, 'my name is Edward Todd.'

Chapter Thirteen

Chris could have died when he heard the name; how could this be? Of all the people he had passed on his walk, and even in the smoky tavern, why did he have to bump into Emily's brother. He had hoped that he may just be another man with the same name, but the way things were going, and the way that events had already unravelled, he just knew deep down that this was indeed the notorious villain that Emily had described to him.

'Could you lend me a shilling or two, my new-found friend?' Ed asked, placing his grubby arm firmly around Chris's shoulder. 'And don't say you ain't got any; I saw you bring out a few shillings out that there pocket.'

There were sympathetic glances from other people standing nearby, they obviously had heard of, or knew, Ed Todd. Chris obligingly sat on a long bench among all the other diners and promptly, though somewhat carefully, tucked into his pie. A sip of his ale should have forewarned him of what was to come; the beer was barely drinkable, the pie however tasted tough and out of date, if such a concept existed in those times. Ed sat drooling over the pie that Chris was picking at, so Chris obliged the hungry man and shoved it over in his direction. He then dipped deep into his pockets and gave what looked like a shilling to Ed, then made his excuses and got up to leave.

A sharp pull on his left hand drew him back towards the dishevelled villain. Ed held tight to Chris's wrist as he looked him straight in his eyes.

'Thank you,' he said, letting his iron grip loosen somewhat. 'We shall meet again.'

'No doubt,' Chris replied, eager to get to the door and leave that particular dwelling. He glanced back toward the tavern as he walked away, mainly to check to see if Ed was following him or not. But this time, at least, he was safe.

It was on his walk back to the Doctor's that he started

observing his new surroundings. Some of the older, wooden-structured buildings seemed to be so close to each other that neighbours, leaning out of bedroom windows could hang out their washing on lines that stretched from house to house and chat to one another. He noticed chimney sweeps leaving houses, with their little boy helpers next to them, all black from head to toe. Sanitation hardly seemed a priority, as some people overtly relieved themselves in the streets after leaving various hostelries. He passed an old blacksmith's workplace, and couldn't help but peep in to see a true craftsman at work.

Glancing up at a bridge overhead, he could not help but notice the amazing engineering that had gone into building such a superb structure. His eyes on the beautiful arches just as a steam train rattled past overhead. How could he have been so oblivious to all of this; he must have been deep in thought to not even notice; this was Industrial Revolution history at its best, and he was actually living it.

Flower sellers and all other types of peddlers littered the streets, pestering the gentry in hope of making a daily crumb. A pretty little matchstick girl caught his eye, and he headed over toward her. She was so scruffy, her hair uncombed and her face grubby; she looked like she hadn't eaten for a week.

'How much, little girl?' Chris enquired.

'Halfpenny a box,' she replied. He felt so sorry for the girl, and for some reason she looked familiar to him. 'Here, young lady,' he said, handing over a shilling, and taking the matches out of her hand. 'Listen to me,' he whispered, handing over a penny. 'You put the penny in the box and the shilling in your own pocket and that will be our secret, and we will tell no one.' He put his finger to his lips. The girl was overwhelmed with gratitude. Chris was just about to walk away when she called him back; he turned toward her and she took hold of his hand and kissed it. 'Thank you sir,' she whispered, putting her own finger to her lips: 'our secret.' Chris was almost overcome with emotion as he left the girl and walked on. He took a brief glimpse back, and saw her in the distance still smiling in her gratitude.

Crossing the road was even more dangerous than it was in 2008. At least then he knew which direction the traffic was coming from. After safely negotiating a crossing he continued his walk back. The nearer he got to the Doctor's house, the more affluent the town and its people seemed to be; the homes were grander, and the people more elegantly attired, although scruffy little street urchins and pickpockets still hovered in the shadows. He noticed how sickly some of these unfortunate children looked. Many of them looked so pale and thin that he felt sure that a long life would certainly elude them.

The nearing sight of Dr Mayfield's house had never seemed so comforting. Chris was tired after his long walk, but although weary and confused, he felt his mind was a little clearer, and he himself was a bit closer to coming to terms with his fate.

If he had felt happy in the least, the stern greeting of Maud Johnson at the front door jolted him quickly back to reality.

'You are wearing the good Doctor out,' she snapped in greeting. 'I did warn you that if you hurt the Doctor, you would have me to deal with.'

Fortunately for Chris, Dr Mayfield entered the conversation when he did. He promptly and sternly told Maud that Chris was no trouble, and was welcome, and that she would make sure of that.

'Please come in, Christopher,' the Doctor asked.

Chris duly followed the man into his study, and told him that he was slowly reconciling himself to his fate.

The Doctor kindly offered Chris lodgings for as long as he needed, and told him that there was much that they could learn from each other. Chris thanked the man and agreed. However, the Doctor's smiles of happiness quickly evaporated as Chris told him that he had met Ed Todd in the tavern. He agreed that of all the people around, it was strange that he should bump into him.

Chris also told the Doctor about the matchstick girl, and how he thought that he recognised her, although he could not remember from where.

'This is not a coincidence,' the Doctor assured Chris. 'Somehow, somewhere, something is going to happen, and it is going to involve you, Christopher,' he sternly continued. 'We must be ready for whatever fate throws at us; we must be ready.'

Chapter Fourteen

Chris took heed of the Doctor's words, for he knew deep down that he was right. The way events had turned out already, it was as though history had already been written, and he was just there acting out the scenes.

He retired to his room for the evening. He hadn't even got his shirt off when Emily crept into his room. He was so glad to see her that not one word passed between them; they just embraced and then kissed. Chris took a firm hold of Emily as he passionately threw her on the bed; he caressed her quivering body, while undressing her. He gently kissed her from her feet to her head, and then they made beautiful love. Afterwards they lay side by side, facing each other, offering the occasional loving kiss. Chris was thinking about the day he had had; he contemplated telling Emily the bad news that her brother was out of prison, and that he had met him. But he did not want to spoil the moment, so he thought the news would keep.

'Can I stay the night, Chris?' Emily asked tenderly. 'Please?'

'But you will be missed,' Chris replied.

'Oh no, Christopher,' Emily answered, 'no one will know that I am here, and I will leave before anyone else wakes up,' she continued. She went on to explain to Chris that, for some unexplained reason, she had been having bad feelings that something was going to happen, and that the last time she had had feelings of this kind was when she had dreamt that she had met Chris out in the Fens, on the night that he had actually shown up.

'Very well,' Chris agreed, 'that would be lovely.' The happy couple made love once more then tenderly fell asleep in each other's arms.

Chris drifted into his slumber and directly into a dream. This time he was not in hospital but back in his own home. Jane was there; Chris's parents were not, but two other figures lingered in the background. As their faces became more visible to Chris he discovered that it was Jane's parents. There was dialogue, but he could not make out what was being said. It was like he was losing his connection with 2008, everything seemed to be going in and out of focus. The only words that he could make out was Jane's father telling her, 'We are here for you, Jane.' Then it was just as if somebody had pulled out the plug, because everything went dark, blank in fact; try as he could, Chris could not focus. He could see nothing but black.

He woke up sweating profusely.

'What is it, my love?' a tired Emily asked.

'Just a bad dream, my love, you go back to sleep.'

Chris lay awake for a few moments, still holding on to Emily. He could feel her breath as she gently exhaled softly into his face. She looked so beautiful and content, so deliriously happy, and he could see that she felt safe in his arms. In fact he too felt safe in her arms; she at least was the only thing that felt real in this living nightmare. He closed his eyes, safe in the knowledge that she would be there for him when he woke. For the first time in days he did not feel alone.

The thick, dark curtains had blacked out the night and the dense fog that lingered outside. He heard the loud cry of the night watchman, calling out the hour, 'Three o'clock and all is well.' He snuggled closer and drifted back into his slumber.

A sweet tender kiss aroused Chris from his sleep, as Emily whispered, 'I must be getting back to my room before old Maud taps on my door, and discovers that I am missing.'

She dressed, and kissed her lover once more before tucking him up, telling him, 'You sleep some more, my love,' and quietly leaving the room.

Once awake, sleep was the last thing on Chris's mind as once again a thousand and one thoughts raced through his head. He knew that he had to talk some more to the Doctor; he was the only one who knew what was going on. He tried to come to terms with his apparent death in 2008. At least he had Emily, and if things did not, as he feared, turn out bad, then he and Emily could make it and live happily ever after.

For the first time in days he was starting to think positively;

there were still plenty of negatives, but at least now he realised that he had no control over his situation. He resolved to make the most of 1898; at least, if fate did not throw too many bad cards at him, he may have some control.

As daylight came Chris got up and headed to his bowl of water for a wash; hardly the warm, invigorating shower that he was used to, but that was then and this is now he thought. He made the most of the cold water and hard, unscented soap; at least it woke him up.

At least he did not have to wake up the Doctor, or interrupt him for that matter; the Doctor was up and seemingly anxious to speak to Chris. He was waiting patiently in the hallway as Chris walked down the grand staircase.

'Let us walk,' the Doctor suggested; putting on his coat and top hat, he offered Chris a spare coat of his and also a top hat. 'So you look a part of this era,' he quipped. Chris just laughed, and accepted the man's generosity.

A thick blanket of fog greeted them as they walked through the front door. Chris noticed as he was walking the smoke billowing out of chimneys from every house; this only contributed to the dense fog that lingered and polluted the air. Horse-drawn carts delivered coal to each of the houses, with young scruffy kids accompanied by their mothers, or out-of-work fathers, picking up the fallen pieces and placing them in buckets. These were obviously the less comfortable, or the lower class. These scenes of poverty struck a chord with Chris, who had never before witnessed such deprivation.

It was literally hard to see a hand in front of you, let alone somebody in the distance, but the Doctor managed it.

'Recognise that man, Christopher?' the Doctor asked. Chris strained to see, but at best could only see a faint shadow.

'No,' he replied, still straining,

'Well, that figure over there, Christopher, is Ed Todd.'

Chris looked stunned, 'Are you sure?' he asked.

Dr Mayfield gave a knowing nod of his head. 'That is why I was not too surprised when you told me that you had seen him.' The Doctor continued: 'He has been there for the past two days now, watching, waiting, before making his move.' Chris was taken aback by this; although he felt sure their paths would cross once more, he had hoped it would not be so soon. He feared immediately for his lover, Emily. Bad thoughts crossed his mind.

'We should tell Sergeant Thomas,' Chris said in desperation. The Doctor just nodded once more and tugged Chris away, so as not to arouse suspicion.

'We must not let him know that we know he is there,' the Doctor said, tapping the side of his nose with his forefinger. 'Come, we must walk on and plan our course of action, if we are to stay one step ahead of the game.' The two men strode side by side, pondering Edward Todd's next move.

Chapter Fifteen

The dense fog did not seem to be clearing at all as the morning rush of horse-drawn carriages got underway. The fog did not seem to deter them at all, and the traffic chaos built up.

The two men decided that their course of action would be to let Sergeant Thomas know about it all. Although Todd was committing no offence by just loitering around, both Chris and the Doctor knew something was afoot.

'He's what?' bellowed the gruff Welsh voice of Sergeant Thomas. 'I only put that blackguard away three years ago, what is wrong with society.' He looked sternly into the eyes of Chris and said: 'We need your full co-operation on this one sonny.'

Chris knew what he had to do. 'You want me to go undercover?' he replied.

'What?' shouted Sergeant Thomas, even louder than before. 'Are you a bloody coward; is this what they taught you in London? You can't hide under the covers boy, you got to go out and reel him in towards us.' Chris chuckled to himself; obviously the Sergeant hadn't heard of undercover work. 'I understand, Sergeant,' Chris replied: 'What do you want me to do?'

'Nothing,' Sergeant Thomas answered; 'judging by what you have told me, he will find you.'

Chris reluctantly agreed, although he could feel his stomach churning at the thought.

The two left the police station, with Thomas's voice still ringing out. 'Franklin! Get that bloody dog out of here.'

Heading back toward what was now home, the Doctor explained to Chris that he would not be around that evening, as he had a prior engagement. Chris did not like to pry, so decided to keep quiet; anyway, he thought, what concern was it of his, what Dr Mayfield got up to in his spare time.

He need not have worried, because the Doctor explained anyway. He told Chris that he was in the process of writing a book on mediums and psychics, from a very sceptical point of view. He had in the past written several papers on the matter; he would attend so-called séances, and invariably expose these people as the frauds that they were.

It was his private work of hypnosis that had got him into this; the regression of several of his subjects, drifting back to a previous existence, aroused his curiosity. He had hoped to discover a genuine medium, but to date he had not. This frustrated the Doctor a great deal. He felt that he had evidence that people did live, die, and were reborn, but his quest to find a genuine medium to substantiate his findings so far drew blanks. 'So who's the unfortunate fake tonight?' Chris enquired.

'Elisabeth Schneider; she is a German lady who has resided in these parts for the past seven years.' The Doctor chuckled as he continued: 'Everything is German these days.'

'Trust me,' Chris replied, 'in sixteen years' time it won't be.'

'You should come,' the Doctor suggested. 'Yes,' he continued, scratching his grey whiskers, 'surely that would be the ultimate test; if she cannot pick up anything from you, that is another night ruined.'

Chris thought about it. He really did want a night with Emily, especially as her rogue brother was now back on the scene; but he could see the excitement in the Doctor's eyes, and how could he refuse the man that had helped him and believed in him?

'Very well,' he replied, 'I shall come with you.'

Chris had tea with the Doctor while discussing the night's events. Emily served them. A loving glance was exchanged between the two, plainly obvious to the Doctor's canny eyes. Chris was amazed by the beautiful china tea service; he was more used to a tea bag in a mug. This was all so elegant; what a shame, he thought, that although civilisation had progressed vastly, it had lost so many of the old, elegant Victorian values.

Emily poured the tea, her eyes still focused on the love of her life. She was about to leave the two gentlemen to carry on their discussion, when the Doctor grabbed her hand and gently pulled her toward him. Tapping his knee with his left hand, he gestured Emily to sit on his knee. She trustingly obliged.

'This is my prize possession, Christopher,' he said rather

sternly. 'I took the child in at fourteen, and now she is a very beautiful young lady, don't you agree, Christopher?' he continued.

'Yes, sir, she is,' Chris nervously replied. 'If you are serious about her, Christopher,' the Doctor went on, 'then I am of the old-fashioned variety; it is me you must ask for her hand in marriage.'

Chris just sat mouth agape; he did not know what to say. He briefly looked at Emily, who was smiling uncomfortably.

'Well, Christopher?' the Doctor asked, tapping his fingers on the arm of the chair.

Chris exhaled a very nervous cough, 'Well, sir,' he stuttered, 'could I please have the hand in marriage of your legal guardian, er, sir?'

The Doctor smiled; he rose to his feet and warmly shook Chris by the hand. 'You may, my son, yes you may.' Chris and Emily embraced, and the caring Doctor placed his arms around the two of them.

A loud scream of joy came from beyond the door. 'Yes, you may come in too, Johnson,' the Doctor shouted out. Maud Johnson, usually the stern, outspoken spinster, rushed into the study and joined them in their embrace. 'Well, that will make it legal, and stop you having to tiptoe into the room,' she blurted out.

The Doctor gave Maud a stern look, but could not keep up the appearance, so he too burst into laughter. 'We shall book the church a week on Saturday,' the Doctor enthused. 'Should not be a problem; don't get too many weddings in January.'

Chris at first was quite shocked at the haste in which the Doctor wanted to arrange the wedding. That would only give them a little over a week. But he anticipated the Doctor's thoughts, that firstly he wanted Emily to be settled and safe, and secondly he did not know if Chris was likely to disappear back into 2008, although he doubted the possibility, as the Christopher in 2008 was dead. But nevertheless, he was happy to have him here in 1898.

'I shall see to the arrangements first thing,' he told them. 'And Johnson, you will help me,' the Doctor added.

'Yes, sir,' Maud replied, still smiling with joy for her colleague.

The Doctor told Emily and Maud to go and have a chat and prepare for the future, while he and Christopher discussed their plan for the evening.

Chapter Sixteen

Christopher pulled open the gate which led to the front door of Elisabeth Schneider's house. The dense fog had not lifted. A tall, well-dressed gentleman answered the door. He had been expecting the Doctor, and warmly shook his hand and offered to take his hat and coat. 'And you must be…?' the gentleman asked, with his hand outstretched for Christopher to shake. 'Now why would he want to tell you that,' the Doctor chipped in before Chris had a chance to offer a reply.

The gentleman shook Chris's hand and said: 'Well, my name is Chester; now, may I take your coat and hat sir?'

Chris removed his coat, and he and the Doctor were shown into the next room. It was a large living room, with a high ceiling; the gas lanterns were turned down low, and Chris saw a large oblong table with various grim-looking people already at their places. Chris sat down where he was shown. The Doctor, however, was busy looking around the room for any props that he could find; he lifted the tablecloth that adorned the table, and peered underneath for any other clues. Satisfied that there was nothing untoward, the Doctor took his place at the table next to Chris. The gaslights were turned off, and four strategically placed candles were lit.

A sharp intake of breath could be heard as Elisabeth Schneider entered the room. There were twelve other people at the table, as well as Chris and the Doctor, and they all, with the exception of Dr Mayfield, looked overwhelmed and anxious as their host sat down.

Elisabeth must have been in her sixties: if she wasn't, then she certainly looked like she was; her hair was pure white, while the wrinkles on her weathered face told a story in themselves. She wore a long, dark brown dress, and had a cream crocheted shawl over her shoulders. She peered over her glasses, and asked everyone to link hands, and think of any deceased loved ones.

Elisabeth scanned the table of expectant guests, and then slowly closed her eyes. Her head twisted a little and her face seemed to be contorting.

'Oh, my chest,' she whispered in a different voice; 'it is so tight I can not breathe.'

'That was my Harold!' a voice came from the other end of the table.

'Harold, it's Mary; are you all right, my dear?' she bellowed out.

'Yes, I am fine, Mary,' the voice replied: 'I am in no more pain, I can breathe again now; I just want you to know that I am happy and at peace.'

'Balderdash!' the Doctor shouted, banging his fist on the table. 'That woman told you her name, and let's face it: who can actually breathe when they are taking their last breath?'

'Please, Dr Mayfield,' Chester pleaded. 'Please allow Miss Elizabeth the grace to continue.'

Dr Mayfield nodded his head by means of an apology. He realised he had been a little hasty in his condemnation of the medium. Elisabeth Schneider continued her trance, and called out various different names; some of them meant something to her audience, while many others passed without remark.

At last she took a deep breath and slumped into her chair, her chin almost on her chest. The guests were still holding hands; all except the Doctor, who was drumming his fingers on the table, much to the annoyance of the others. He was readying himself to jump up and expose the medium as yet another fraud when she uttered, 'Christopher.' It was a faint whisper, but Chris heard it and his eyes opened wide; his head tilted to one side as he looked directly at Elisabeth Schneider.

'Christopher,' she whispered again, 'it's Jane; please don't give in, please fight.' Chris had tears rolling down his face. He tried to control himself, but he was overwhelmed. The Doctor by now had stopped his incessant tapping, and was using his fingers to prod Chris into asking questions, to start a dialogue.

Chris wiped his eyes and stuttered out a few words; 'Jane, it's Chris: where are you?' The medium opened her eyes; her pupils were nowhere in sight and only the whites of her eyes could be seen. She turned her blind gaze in the direction of Chris.

'You are lost,' she told him. 'Your soul is lost, your heart is found; time stands between you and Jane.'

Chris was almost speechless, but again egged on by the Doctor he asked, 'Is Christopher dead? Where is Christopher?'

She replied: 'You are here, and you are still there.' Chris was trying to regain his composure when the medium blurted out: 'Danger, danger before you wake.' Her head then slumped forward, hitting the table with some force. Chester ran over to her and hoisted her back into her chair; he was forcing her to sip water, as she started to come back round.

Dr Mayfield sat motionless; he was not the type to get overexcited, but as he held his hands on his portly belly Chris could see that he was affected by what the medium had said.

'It was all rather vague though,' the Doctor said, looking in the direction of Elisabeth Schneider and Chester. Chris, still amazed and confused by what he had heard, wondered to himself just exactly what the Doctor would write about in his report. There has been quite a lot of waffle, but what she told Chris, vague or not, was enough to convince him.

Chris asked Elisabeth if she could help him any more. 'It's no good, young man,' Chester interrupted. 'When she comes out of a trance she remembers nothing.'

This did not help Chris at all. He had heard enough to set his mind wandering. As he and the Doctor set off on their journey back, Chris was convinced that his life – and maybe Emily's – was in danger that very night.

The horse-drawn carriage rocked from side to side on the road to the Doctors' house. 'You can't take it literally, Christopher, what Elisabeth Schneider said,' spoke the Doctor, breaking the silence.

'She knew who I was,' Christopher replied. 'How, how could she have known?' The Doctor just shrugged. He did not know the answers either, and he too was concerned.

'I would like Emily to stay in your room tonight, Christopher,' he said, bringing a smile to Chris's face. 'You can sleep in the armchair, do you hear?' he continued, winking as he said it. Chris nodded, and smiled back at the Doctor, thankful for the opportunity to protect Emily.

Chapter Seventeen

Chris bid the good Doctor goodnight and headed for his room. He sat in the armchair facing the window, staring out at the dense fog which was still lingering. He thought of looking outside, to see if he could spot Ed Todd, but he was too scared of what he might see.

He sat there pondering what Elisabeth Schneider had said. Was he still alive in 2008; could she have meant that, when she said, he was not dead? He replayed every word the medium had uttered over and over again in his head.

When Emily entered the room, he could not have been more pleased to see her. He embraced her tenderly, but more firmly than he ever had before.

They sat together on the edge of the bed. Emily was so excited about the wedding; she was going to get her dress the next day, she informed Chris, and he was to take her on Monday to choose her ring.

Events were happening so fast Chris could hardly keep up. He tried to share Emily's enthusiasm, and while deep down he did, he could not hide the fact that he was scared to go to sleep. *Danger, before you wake*; the words of the medium were playing on his mind. He decided to try to match Emily's enthusiasm; at least that way his mind was off whatever perils lay ahead.

She looked deep into his eyes. 'You do love me, Christopher,' she quietly spoke, 'do you not?'

'With all my heart, Emily, and for as long as I live,' he lovingly replied. He held out his arms and placed his hands on her shoulders. 'I love you dearly,' he whispered.

After lengthy discussions about their big day a little over a week away, they were both overcome with tiredness. With what bit of energy they had left they made love, and both fell asleep in a fond embrace.

Chris slipped into his dream once more; again, he was in a

room, but all he could see were Jane and her parents. He soon realised that he was in his own apartment.

He heard Jane asking, 'What are we going to do, Mum, why us? Why did this have to happen to us? I will never forgive myself.' Then it was as if someone had turned down the volume. Everything became blurred and hazy, and then very distant; it was just like a camera was panning out, until Jane and her parents were no more than dots at the end of a very long tunnel.

Although still asleep, Chris was trying desperately to get back into the dream, but he couldn't. A loud bang roused him from his slumber; he woke in a panic and turned to see if Emily was all right. She was still fast asleep, and looked so peaceful and content that he did not like to wake her. He lay next to her, stroking her hair. His eyes scanned the dark room; he tried to control his breathing for fear of being heard if somebody was in the room. Quietly and deliberately he slid the bedclothes away, and one leg after the other he softly got out of bed. Making his way toward the bedroom door, he grabbed an ornament off his bedside table and tiptoed toward the direction of where he thought he had heard the sound. Before he could reach the door it swung open, almost knocking him over; he stretched out his left hand to ward off his intruder, while lifting the ornament above his head ready to strike whoever it was bursting in.

'Good God, Christopher, what are you doing?' a startled Doctor asked.

'Dear God, I am sorry,' a very shocked and nervous Chris replied. 'I thought that Ed Todd had broken in.'

He explained to the Doctor that he had woken to a loud bang, and fearing the worst he had armed himself to protect Emily. 'The noise you heard was Sergeant Thomas, demonstrating his primitive methods of dealing with villains,' the Doctor explained, now starting to see the funny side of things. 'When you're dressed you should come down and hear his plan of action; that's what I came up to tell you,' he continued, smiling to himself, his chubby round face now breaking into a hearty laugh.

'I suppose I should have knocked, but I did not wish to wake Emily; and knowing that you would be in the armchair, I thought I could wake you without disturbing her. Good to see that you are alert and able to protect her,' he finished, closing the door behind him.

'Is everything all right, Christopher?' Emily asked sweetly, still rubbing her tired eyes.

'Yes, yes my love,' he replied, 'you go back to sleep. I've to speak with Dr Mayfield, then I shall return.' He gently kissed her on the cheek, stroked her hair from her face, and then got dressed himself.

It wasn't until he got downstairs that he noticed that it was a little after three o'clock. He wondered to himself what the urgency was. He was greeted by the weathered face of Sergeant Thomas. He was holding a huge stick in his hand that resembled a baseball bat of the twentieth century. He had been demonstrating its use when he accidentally hit the door with his chosen weapon of violence. That explained the noise that had woken Chris up. But why the early morning meeting Chris wondered.

Thomas explained that time was of the essence, and that as Edward Todd was still loitering with menace around the area, he suspected that the Doctor's house, or even Emily, would be his target. So Sergeant Thomas had done what he did best, and that was to act on impulse, seize the moment and go to see Dr Mayfield there and then.

'First thing, Christopher, you will go out and bump into your *friend*,' the enthusiastic Sergeant explained, 'and then earn his trust and find out his plans.'

Chris did not like the sound of this; he had thought he would have to deal with Ed Todd, but not like this, and not so soon. But he did want to protect Emily and the good Doctor, who had done so much to help him, so he agreed.

He endured the iron grip of the gruff Sergeant's handshake, and then made his way back up the stairs to bed. He had no doubts that he wouldn't sleep, so he sat in the armchair, lovingly watching over Emily and contemplating the day ahead.

Chapter Eighteen

Chris took early morning tea with the Doctor; he did not even think to tell the Doctor of his dream the previous night, and instead the conversation was all about how Chris should get whatever information he could from Ed Todd. But it was of the utmost importance that his own safety was assured: he did after all, have a wedding to attend in a week's time.

Chris took to the early morning air. The dense fog that had lingered over the last two days was now starting to lift, and a light drizzle filled the air. It wasn't long before Chris spotted Ed Todd. This time he had another man with him: a short, balding, stocky fellow, oddly dressed in various colours that didn't match. He was somewhat shorter than Ed, although he looked very much his equal in the villainy stakes.

Chris had deliberately taken as little money out with him as possible, fearing that the scrounging Ed may demand more off him this time. He could feel his stomach churning, he could sense the danger. The very thought of making contact with these vagabonds scared him; so it hardly bore thinking about what destiny had in store for him.

He took a deep breath and painted a plastic smile over his troubled face as he headed for the pair.

'Ed!' he shouted as he crossed the road, pretending to be surprised. 'Remember me?' A scowl was aimed in his direction, as the surprised Ed scanned the oncoming man, wondering whether to stay and confront him or beat a hasty retreat.

Fortunately for Chris, Ed recognised him and after a moment his frown turned into an almost welcoming smile.

'It's Christopher, ain't it?' he replied, holding out his grubby hand for Chris to shake. 'This is my good acquaintance, Charlie,' he told Chris, promptly elbowing the man in the ribs to be polite and shake the hand of Chris. 'He is not so skilled in the school of manners, is my mate Charlie,' Ed continued, 'but he's a damn good man to have around, know what I mean Christopher?' Ed shouted, aiming a playful punch to the ribs of Chris. Chris just gulped, grateful that Ed had no intentions of connecting with the punch; the wind force and sheer speed behind it was powerful enough.

'So what brings you round these parts, Ed?' Chris asked, trying to find out whatever he could.

Ed placed a well-muscled arm around Chris's shoulder and, trusting his new friend, explained – in part, at least – what he was doing there. He told Chris that as he had not long been released from prison, he had no chance of getting a job, and in reality did not want one anyway, so he was looking for large houses, preferably in this affluent area, with intentions of robbery.

He would, he said, quite often stake out a target in order to gain a rough idea of times when the residents would be out, or their bedtime habits, if a night raid was more appropriate. With his arm still firmly around Chris's shoulder, Ed spun him around in the direction of the Doctor's house. Chris felt his knees go weak; his worst nightmare seemed to be happening right before his very eyes.

'That one,' Ed said, pointing in the appropriate direction. 'You see, Christopher,' he continued, pulling Chris toward him so that his low, overpowering voice was reducing to a whisper, 'I have reasons for wanting to do that there house, one because it has a lot of valuable items in there. But two, and the most important of all,' he whispered, now grinning with excitement, 'well, let's just say I have a bit of insurance in there.' Ed laughed out loud, and turned to face Charlie, who obligingly laughed along with his accomplice; after all he didn't dare not to.

Chris tried desperately to control himself; he could feel the fear and dread bubbling up inside of him. 'When, Ed?' he dared to ask.

'Don't know yet,' Ed replied, quick as a flash, 'but soon, very soon, because I ain't got any money.' He laughed once more, once again looking at Charlie for his backup laugh.

Chris knew he had to do something; he knew that if he did not know the exact time and date of Ed's planned manoeuvres, then he had little or no chance of protecting Emily. Although Ed had not mentioned her by name, or even said that he had a sister in there for that matter, Chris knew exactly what Ed meant by his insurance quip.

Trying desperately to gain a little trust from the two villains, Chris told them that he knew the insides of the house, how to gain the easiest access, and exactly what was worth taking.

This did gain the interest of Ed. 'Go on,' he demanded, rubbing his hands like a demented demon.

Chris went on to explain that the Doctor was a friend of his father's, and, thinking quickly, added that he despised the man ever since his little sister had died because of Dr Mayfield. Chris tried desperately to have an evil look on his face, at least one that could try to match theirs, as he spoke his fibs telling of his loathing and utter distrust of the Doctor.

He begged Ed to let him in on the job. 'I know that you hardly know me,' Chris said, 'but I do have good reason to want revenge on that man, and I ask for nothing,' he continued. This pleased Ed, but puzzled him also; as he scratched his chin with his grubby hands, before he could ask the obvious question Chris jumped in. 'Revenge on that Doctor, would be reward enough for me.'

Ed knew that if what Chris was saying was true, then this broadened his chances greatly. Chris told Ed that he was not rich, but that his father was quite well off, so it wasn't the money that he would be doing it for, solely the aforementioned revenge. To Chris's relief and astonishment, Ed bought his story.

He told Chris to meet up with him and Charlie at eight o'clock at the Bell Tavern, in order to plan when they were going to strike. Chris accepted their invitation, and turned to walk away.

'Chris!' Ed shouted. 'Seeing as you are so well off and all, how's about lending me and Charlie a shilling or two for some food.'

Chris dug deep into his pocket, and brought out a shilling, Ed winked and smiled at Chris; if he did not look rough enough already the fact that a few of his teeth were missing made him look even more so. The few remaining ones looked rotten, and his breath could wilt fresh-blossomed flowers. Nevertheless, Chris had to endure these unpleasantries if he was to get all the information needed to recapture these villains.

As Chris walked over the busy main road he heard Ed scream out his name and order him not to be late. He nodded and waved, then watched the two disappear in the distance before he safely made his way to see Sergeant Thomas.

Chapter Nineteen

Hurrying over to the police station, Chris took one last look behind him to make sure that Ed and Charlie were out of sight; having come this far, he did not want to run the risk of ruining everything.

A pleasant Constable Franklin greeted Chris on his entrance to the police house; he gave an encouraging wink as he went off to fetch the less pleasant Sergeant Thomas.

The familiar gruff voice of Thomas echoed around the room as he ordered Chris to sit down. 'Well,' he asked, 'have you made contact; if so what do you know? I take it you're not here for no reason.'

Chris explained to Sergeant Thomas all that had happened, and informed him that he was due to meet Ed and Charlie that evening at the Bell Tavern.

Sergeant Thomas warned Chris to be very careful; he knew of Ed Todd's violent background, and his accomplice wasn't much nicer either. He told Chris to see them at the tavern, but not to go anywhere with them; as long as he was in a public place he should be safe.

The two men discussed at great length Ed's potential plans, and decided that Chris must try to convince Ed to be precise with his timing, for as persistent as he was as a burglar, he was also very spontaneous with it; he struck when and where he wanted. This time, if they were to catch him they needed to know when he was going to act. They did not need to follow him inside to catch him in the act: oh no, this was not 2008. Things were certainly different in 1898; they only needed Ed to be caught in the area with the tools of his trade, and that alone would be enough to arrest and charge him, followed of course by the obligatory beating.

The Sergeant ended his chat with Chris by telling him that he must find out if they intended to use guns. Chris just shuddered at the thought.

He left Sergeant Thomas, bid his farewell to Constable Franklin, patted his trusted dog and set about making his way to the Doctor's house, where no doubt he would be obliged to go through the whole story again. The long morning's events had worn Chris out; he was looking forward to seeing Emily and just being able to hold her.

The Doctor seemed pleased with what Chris had told him. He thought the story that Chris had invented, of the Doctor being a friend of his father's, quite brilliant.

He looked earnestly into the eyes of Chris, and his jolly round face took on a more serious look about it. 'We shall have to make sure that we are ready for his every move,' he stated. Chris just nodded in agreement, and promised the Doctor that he would find out and try to be a part of every last detail of Ed's plans; and, of course, to thwart his evil intentions.

Emily was very much on Chris's mind, and the Doctor could see that, so, safe in the knowledge that Chris had matters in hand, he excused the man to spend what was left of the day with Emily. Before Chris left the room, the Doctor blurted out 'Oh I almost forgot,' Chris turned back to listen to his friend.

'The wedding,' the Doctor began. His face once more was assuming its usual round smile. 'It is to be next Saturday, a week today, at midday at Saint Peter's church.' Chris felt all of his fears and anxieties subside as his thoughts now focused on his beautiful day, and the even more beautiful Emily. The Doctor informed him that Emily and Maud had been out that very morning looking for a wedding dress, while he had taken care of the church arrangements.

'We shall have to attend church tomorrow,' the Doctor informed Chris. This was in fact normal practice for almost everybody in the town, and one that the Doctor kept up, and insisted that his staff keep up also. Chris, not being well, had missed out on the previous visit, much to his relief, as he did not possess one religious bone in his body. However, the strange events that had happened to him during the last week had now opened his mind somewhat: as he left the good Doctor to his planning and walked out of the room, it even occurred to him to try to offer a prayer; what harm could it do, he thought.

The early morning drizzle had now turned into a heavy downpour and the dark skies shrouded the early evening; but the inclement January weather did not deter Chris and Emily from their stroll. He wanted to be able to be with her alone, and spend a little time to discuss their wedding plans, before he had to go and meet Ed. The loving duo walked hand in hand, looking forward with excitement to their pledged union. Chris held his brolly high in an effort to keep both himself and Emily dry from the deluge that was raging down on them. After much discussion they headed back in the direction of the house. It was then that Chris decided to tell Emily of his plans for later that evening, to meet her villainous brother. She quickly realised that nothing she could say would deter him from his moral obligation, so she unwillingly gave her blessing for the rendezvous.

The trappings of the age were no longer a mystery to Chris now; he had outgrown his shock at the details of life in Victorian times. In fact, he now felt such a part of it all that every time he went out he almost took his surroundings for granted.

They weren't far from home, however, when something unfamiliar to that era caught his eye. At first he could not make it out, but a brilliant light, sunbeam-like, shone just opposite them on the other side of the road; in fact it was both light and sunny over on that side. A quick glance at the sky assured Chris that it was still black with rain clouds, and heavy rain teemed down from them; yet just over the road it was bright.

'Look at that,' Chris said, pointing over the road.

'At what, my love?' Emily replied, busily trying to brush the rain from her eyes to see what had caught the attention of Chris. He just stood motionless as he stared into the light; at first it was just a bright day to him over the road, until he noticed that all of the people and the buildings behind were actually of his era; he was staring at 2008.

A blinding light penetrated Chris's eyes, as a headache that he could only describe as a nuclear explosion overwhelmed him, and then all went black.

Emily screamed for help as Chris passed out and hit the cobbled street. She ran to the house for help, and within seconds Dr Mayfield and Albert were standing over him.

Chapter Twenty

Fortunately for Chris, he had been only yards from the house when he blacked out.

He came to once again on the Doctor's sofa, to find the Doctor, Maud, Albert, and a very upset and concerned Emily standing by him.

'What happened?' he asked.

'You had a relapse, Christopher,' the Doctor informed him. 'Nothing more; you will be OK.'

Chris waited for the others to leave the room before he told the Doctor what he had seen.

The Doctor listened intently to Chris, but assured him that what he had seen was just a memory of his past, and not a reality. It was more than likely brought on by the stress of the day's events, coupled with the fear of meeting Ed later that evening. 'You must rest,' Dr Mayfield ordered; 'You can not attend your engagement this evening.'

Chris was having none of it. He begged the Doctor to let him go, telling him that he intended to go, with or without his blessing. 'If I do not go,' Chris added, 'then all of your lives are at stake, and possibly mine too.' He convinced the Doctor to let him have an hour's sleep, and then he would be fit to go and keep his appointment.

He went up to his room and lay down on his bed; thankfully, he had Emily with him. Her excuse was that she wanted to nurse him better. She lovingly lay beside him, with her hand pressed tight to a cold, wet flannel on Chris's forehead.

He tried hard to remember what he had seen; could it have been a passage back to 2008, he thought, or was it only a glimpse of what had been; or had he indeed imagined it? One thing was real, and that was his blinding headache. The blackout was also very real, and that frightened him. The time in which he was now living had no way of combating, let alone curing, a brain haemorrhage or any related disorder.

All of these things, in addition to his headache and the dread of meeting Ed Todd, were thwarting his much-needed sleep. The hour in which Chris was supposed to have slept had passed faster than the blinding light which he had seen earlier. Emily gently kissed Chris on his forehead as she removed her hand, and the now-warm flannel.

'Wake up, my love,' she whispered. Chris, although not asleep, did not want to spoil her loving gesture and so gave out a pretend yawn. He stretched out his arms as if waking.

'Thank you, my love,' he whispered back, as he kissed the hand that she had held on his head for an hour long.

The rain had stopped, much to Chris's delight, as a sharp frost now dictated the evening's weather. This was the best thing that could have happened for him, for as he walked, breathing in the cool evening air, he could feel the tension being relieved from his head with every step he took.

A quick glance across the road revealed nothing untoward: he was still in 1898. Maybe he had imagined it after all, he thought. Whether it was due to his experience before he blacked out earlier he did not know, but all of a sudden everything seemed new to him again, and as before he was keenly aware of all of the sights of the era he found himself a part of. The chimneys of every house that he passed billowed out smoke, he wondered what kind of lifestyle the people who dwelled in those houses had. How did they amuse themselves at night; no television or CDs, in fact music had to be played on the local piano, with the family gathered round for a good old singalong. Strange in 2008, but how it must have brought a loving closeness between families; in the more affluent areas; children would have piano or violin lessons.

His thoughts had shortened his journey considerably, but as he had now left the affluence behind him, and was heading deep into the more working class area; then it was the slums. He took the change that he had brought with him, and distributed it around to his pockets, so as not to show Ed that he had more than enough money.

A familiar face then greeted him with an angelic smile; it was his little matchstick girl. She hadn't forgotten her saviour of the day; how could she, for what Chris had given her that day amounted to a small fortune for her. He had been so busy shifting his change into different pockets that he had not noticed her on his approach. Chris stooped down to the young girl's level. 'Hello, my little friend,' he whispered, asking how she was. He could not understand why, yet he felt an overwhelming obligation towards the poor unfortunate girl.

She told him in her best contrived posh accent that she was very well: cold, wet, hungry, but all of that she was used to. Chris wanted to pick her frail frame up and carry her home to safety, but he knew better than to interfere with destiny. However, in his mind he made a pledge to try to help the girl all he could. He asked her why she was out in the rain on such a dreadful evening, and why she was out so late: the time was fast approaching eight o'clock. She explained that she could not return to where she worked, and indeed lodged, until she had sold enough matches to pay for her night's lodgings. The poor girl was an orphan, and was at the mercy of her guardians and employers.

'What is your name child, and how old are you?' Chris politely enquired.

'My name is Lilly, sir,' the girl replied, 'and I think I am twelve.'

Chris could hardly believe it; she looked so small, so malnourished. He thought seven or eight would have been a more appropriate age for her frail-looking body. Staring at the girl once more, he felt once more that he knew her. He scanned the archives of his memory for a clue as to where he knew her from; was it a relative, a friend's daughter? He just could not place her, but her face had left an indelible print on his mind.

'Well, Lilly,' he whispered retrieving a shilling from his pocket, 'this is for you.' And, giving her another penny, he told her that that was for her matches.

With that gesture, he rose to his feet ready to go on to the Bell Tavern. He could see it just across the rain-soaked cobbled street but his attention was pleasantly distracted by Lilly grabbing the back of his hand and gently kissing it.

'Thank you, kind sir,' she whispered, putting her finger to her lips. 'Our little secret.'

Chris gave her matted, scruffy hair a gentle rub with his hand, and smiled as he crossed the road.

He took a deep breath and entered the tavern. As his eyes scanned around the noisy, smoke-filled room for familiar faces, he quickly saw Ed Todd and his scruffy accomplice Charlie sitting quietly at a table in the corner of the room.

Chapter Twenty-One

Ed Todd looked serious; a frown adorned his battle-scarred face. He noticed Chris on his approach, and calmly removed a pocket watch, attached to a chain, from his waistcoat. His eyes rolled down to check the time. 'Ah,' he said breaking out into a somewhat more welcoming smile, 'good to see a man on time, I like that, a man who keeps good time,' he continued. 'Very important in our line of work, eh, Charlie?' he chuckled, elbowing his colleague in the ribs. Charlie gave the obligatory laugh, but before he could form his lips to answer, Ed interrupted: 'Oh well, boys: let's get down to business.' He rubbed his hands together in a motion that suggested that he was well pleased with the way that things were going and he ordered Charlie to fetch Chris a pie and a mug of ale. Charlie nodded and obliged.

Charlie returned with the ale and much to Chris's despair the pie was to follow shortly afterwards. He thanked Charlie for the ale, and got a grunt in return. Ed explained to Chris that Charlie did not say much, being of very poor education and upbringing, and harbouring a deep distrust of everyone except Ed.

'Right then,' Ed turned to business. 'How much do you know about the Doctor's house?'

Chris explained that he had visited the Doctor's house on many occasions. He went on to say that he knew their eating times, their bedtime habits, and even how many locks there were on the front and rear doors. Ed seemed to be taken in by all of this, indeed he was most impressed. 'Windows?' he asked, leaning across the table while rubbing his hand on his stubble.

'The easiest access is the scullery window,' Chris replied. He told the men that the window to the scullery had a weak latch, and was easy to prise open; besides, being at the rear of the building, it posed the least threat of being spotted, especially with the police station being so close by. And to add to that no sleeping quarters were anywhere near, so none of the servants would be aroused should any noise be made.

Ed sat quite still, except for the odd shuffle on his chair when he got excited. Nevertheless, he was taking everything in that Chris was telling him, like the true professional that he was; after all, this was his chosen profession, and one that he was particularly good at.

He looked over at Charlie and said, 'See, doubting Thomas? I told you he would come good.' He then adopted a more serious face and turned his attention back to Chris. 'And valuables,' he added, 'just what is worth lifting in there?'

Chris told him that most of the paintings would be far too large for just the three of them to take; if they needed to make a hasty retreat, then carrying cumbersome items would surely slow them down. He told the two that there was silver in abundance and that the study of the house was where the Doctor kept his money; and, moreover, that there was lots of it as the Doctor had a distinct distrust of banks.

Ed seemed interested in the cash, but the silver caught his interest the most. He asked Chris if the three of them, with two sacks each, would be enough. 'Oh yes,' Chris quickly replied, 'six sacks will be enough.'

Ed was very pleased with what he had heard. He sat at the table and started his planning; even the arrival of the pies did not distract the man from his intense concentration, which did not bother Chris, as his experience with the inedible pies did nothing to raise his appetite. Charlie, however, was already tucking into his.

Ed had worked out how the break-in was going to happen. It was, as Chris had suggested, to be through the scullery window. 'Will we fit through with ease?' Ed asked. Chris now found himself rubbing his own chin in thought; he knew that in reality it would be a struggle and rather slow to get all three of them through without being noticed. But the scullery was where he had been told to direct them by Sergeant Thomas, so as not to endanger anybody's life inside, but also because there was no escape if they were challenged trying to enter at that point. They could not run back because behind them was an eight foot wall, so the only way to run would be straight into the trap that Sergeant Thomas had planned for them.

Chris had to think quickly; he knew the scullery window was in fact too small, but he needed them to try to enter at that point, and as Ed already knew a fair amount about the outside of the building due to his previous few days' reconnaissance, Chris thought it wise to be honest. 'Too small,' he said.

'Thought as much,' Ed replied, and asked Chris if there was any other way. If not, he said they would have to enlist a little helper to aid their entrance. The normal practice would be to get a very small person, or a skinny youngster, normally a child, to enter through the small window then unlock the front or back door for them to quietly and quickly get in.

Ed felt now that Chris was definitely being honest with him. He turned to Charlie and ordered him to go and get the child; in a flash, his accomplice rose from his seat, abandoning his half-eaten pie, and left the tavern to follow the orders of his boss.

'So, when—' Chris began to ask; quick as a flash, and without hesitation, Ed replied: 'Tomorrow night, nine o'clock, sounds good to me after hearing your information.'

This took Chris by surprise; he had hoped that his wedding would take place before Ed's planned break-in, but he knew that this man was extremely dangerous, and the sooner he was caught, the safer everybody would be, especially Emily.

Chris nodded his head in agreement, 'OK, tomorrow it is.'

Ed informed Chris that he would provide the guns and the necessary tools to break in. He and Charlie would keep all of the silver. Chris could have a share in the cash, and the privilege of killing Dr Mayfield if he wished. Again Chris was horrified; he had hoped the use of guns would not be an issue. But he should have known; Ed feared no one, but what he did fear was getting caught and the loss of his liberty. If he had a choice between freedom and killing someone, he would not think twice. Chris was aghast, but nothing could have prepared him for the shock of Charlie's return into the tavern, accompanied by their new accomplice. His face fell as he noticed that the child that Charlie had hand-picked was Lilly, the little matchstick girl.

Chapter Twenty-Two

The look of sheer disappointment that Lilly gave to Chris as Charlie sat her down burned deep into his heart. What could he say to her; he was her hero, her saviour, and now here he was, just another bad man, in the eyes of the child. Chris listened to Ed telling Lilly that tomorrow she was going to help them get into a property; he drilled her about her duties while she just sat taking it all in, still looking at Chris and silently asking why.

It was breaking Chris's heart; he just wanted to hold her frail little frame, and tell her everything would be OK. But he knew that as impossible.

He offered to take her home, so as she would get home safe; that way he thought he could talk to her and assure her that he would personally guarantee her safety, and most of all, that he wasn't really a bad man. But Ed, being the professional that he was, declined Chris's offer. 'Oh no,' he snapped: 'she stays with me and Charlie tonight.' He continued: 'can't have her running and telling the authorities, can we?'

Chris was mortified; one thing he did know, though, was that at least Lilly would be safe, or at least he hoped so. He knew that they needed her for the job, so they would not harm her. That is, unless she tried to run away. All sorts of conflicting thoughts were running through his mind, as Lilly's welfare was now paramount to him.

He had no choice but to leave Lilly in the hands of his two accomplices. It was arranged that they all should meet not far from the Doctor's house at half past eight the following night. Chris gave a last look at the downhearted Lilly, then left for home.

As he got outside the tavern the rain was teeming down even more than before, so he decided to flag down a horse-drawn carriage. Not quite knowing what to do, he decided it wise to observe how someone else did it, and then all he would have to do was simply copy them. An elderly couple raised their arm, and sure enough a carriage pulled up.

Easy, Chris thought. He was just about to put this motion into practice, when the couple asked if he would like to share the carriage with them. He told them where he was going, and they told him in return that they lived just a mile further, so it was on their way. Chris thanked them, and promptly got inside. He sat opposite the couple, both of them well dressed. The lady had a white shawl pulled up over her face, to protect her from the fierce wind and rain, while the gentleman was well groomed in his immaculate top hat and tails. Chris did his best to avoid eye contact, for fear of looking ignorant in front of his generous hosts. It was not until the lady lowered the shawl from her face that he immediately recognised her as Elisabeth Schneider, the medium, and the gentleman accompanying her was Chester. Chris opened his mouth to speak; he was going to say how he recognised them both, but before he could, Elisabeth spoke to him.

'Your danger has not subsided,' she told him. Chris, unable to speak, lowered his eyebrows to an inquiring frown.

'You are going on a journey, short but long; the rights that you do will put right your wrongs. Emily, Jane they are one and the same; so much to lose, so much to gain.'

Chris listened to the old woman; he wondered why she always foretold his fortune in riddle and rhyme. Try as he could, he found it hard to decipher.

'Please, what do you mean?' he asked, still none the wiser. Maybe, he thought, she tells it as she sees it, or as it is given to her; nevertheless he still found it hard to decode. Elisabeth did not answer his question; indeed she seemed totally oblivious to his having said anything at all.

Chester looked kindly at Chris and said, 'There is no more she can tell you, my good friend, she can only say what she sees in her head; I can assure you no more will come tonight.'

A sharp tug on the horse's reins drew the carriage to a halt; Chris had reached his destination. He politely thanked Elisabeth and Chester, and bid them a good night.

His first visit would not be Emily, as much as he wanted it to be; he had a prior engagement with Sergeant Thomas. He kept his appointment, and walked in to see the angry Welshman. 'Are you certain, boy?' he bellowed at Chris.

'Yes,' Chris replied, 'nine o'clock tomorrow night.'

A huge smile spread across the leathery face of the Sergeant, as he thumped his fist loud and hard on the table. He informed Chris as to what he expected him to do, and that was to get himself, Emily and the young girl Lilly out of the way, as he anticipated gunfire.

Chris went over the plan with Sergeant Thomas to make sure that it was perfectly clear to both of them. People's lives were at risk, and he for one did not want to be responsible for anybody losing theirs.

He left the police station, and headed to what was now home; his next task, before he could see Emily, was to brief the Doctor on what was going to happen.

Dr Mayfield was more concerned over Chris's welfare owing to his blackout earlier, but all the same the two discussed the potential plans of Ed, and how they were to thwart his evil attempts.

It was more of an afterthought, but before Chris left Dr Mayfield's study, he told him about meeting Elisabeth Schneider in the carriage on the way home. He told him all about what she had said. The Doctor just rubbed his greying whiskers, and told Chris that what she said, although in riddles, might mean something to them in time to come, but for now they had to concentrate on what was to happen.

A very tired Christopher bid Dr Mayfield goodnight, and went up to bed.

To his delight Emily was waiting for him. As tired as he was from the day's wearying events, he still had the desire and energy to make love to her.

He informed her of what was to happen tomorrow, and assured her that all would be OK.

Although he had more than one concern, the tiredness overwhelmed him and he soon fell asleep, as he hoped that he would, in the arms of the woman he loved.

Chapter Twenty-Three

The beautiful sound of church bells reverberated all around the town as everybody in the house got ready to attend the morning service.

Saint Peter's was a quaint old church, almost a hundred years old so Chris had been reliably informed; it possessed huge grounds and had a beautiful graveyard.

Chris held tight to Emily's hand as they walked behind Dr Mayfield and Maud. Albert strode closely behind them.

The church was full; they all sat at the back, which was the Doctor's usual place, and Chris watched, intent on copying their actions as they bowed to pray.

He found it rather tedious, but took great joy in the comfort that religion brought for these people. Having his own name and Emily's called out 'at this parish' brought it all home to him that in six days' time, he would be marrying Emily in that same church.

All manner of thoughts were racing through Chris's mind; what if Ed and Charlie knew that they were all at the church and he had decided to break in now? If so, would he use Lilly? Would she be all right? Try as he may he could not focus on the service, his mind kept drifting away.

Walking out of the church seemed to take an eternity. Everybody was ambling slowly out, each in turn shaking the vicar's hand and having a brief chat.

Chris was filled with relief when he finally got to the door, only to find that the vicar wanted to chat even longer with him and Emily.

Reverend Arthur Forbes introduced himself to Chris. 'I believe we haven't met before now, Christopher,' he spoke gently in his posh Oxford English accent. 'I shall be conducting your service next week,' he continued. 'It is always a pleasure to see young couples make their vows in front of God.'

Chris smiled politely. 'I am looking forward to it,' he replied, and with that tried to make his exit.

'And you, Emily. I have known you for many years, so I especially take pride in seeing you so happy and content.'

Chris could not believe it; all he wanted to do was rush back and check that the house was OK. After much handshaking and mutual admiration, they eventually managed to leave and catch up with the rest. Then followed a tediously slow walk, with much chat on how lovely the service was; they eventually got back to the house.

Thank God, Chris thought as he entered, and found that all was intact; at least the planned raid was still on for later that evening.

Everybody sat around the table in the Doctors' study, all having a cup of tea and cakes. The pleasant chat revolved around the morning's service and next week's wedding. The look of sheer excitement on Emily's face brought a smile to Chris. She looked so content, and was so full of love to give him for the rest of his life.

Every now and again Dr Mayfield would glance over at Chris; he knew full well what was going through Chris's mind, and he was deliberately trying to keep things as normal as possible for the sake of everybody.

Maud and Emily brought in the Sunday dinner; it was lamb, and the wonderful smell made Chris feel hungrier than he had in ages. They all sat around the table and had a splendid feast.

An afternoon walk did little to calm his nerves, but at least the rain had stopped for a while.

It was a pleasure for Chris as he observed all of the people on their well-earned day of rest. Children flew kites in the park; others were playing with their spinning tops and balls. Families strolled peacefully, occasionally stopping for pleasant chats with neighbours and friends.

Once again Chris fell deep in thought. Emily held tight on to her lover's hand; she now had all she had ever wished for in life. She was in love with a kind, gentle man who adored her too. As they strolled together Chris worried about Lilly; he confided to Emily about her, and explained how worried he was for her welfare. Emily just squeezed harder on his hand.

'It will be all right, my love,' she whispered. Comforting words, but the reality of what could happen was now just a matter of hours away. After a long walk, they at last turned for home. Chris and Dr Mayfield headed straight for the police station, while Maud and Albert took Emily back with them.

Constable Franklin sat calmly stroking his beloved dog, smiling to himself while his superior, Sergeant Thomas grew more irate by the minute. Franklin was a very quiet, almost timid, man. Not much got him wound up, but he did have a good nose for the job. Thomas, however, blundered more than he achieved, mainly because he was so hot-headed. Perhaps as a result, his ferociously scary face bore more battle scars than any man dared to count.

'Well, boy,' he shouted, 'are you ready: are you prepared for tonight?' Chris assured him that he was, and that he was well aware of what he had to do.

'Have you ever used one of these, boy?' Sergeant Thomas growled, handing Chris a gun.

'Good God no,' Chris replied, shying away from the weapon.

'Well, you are going to have to, boy,' he continued. 'It could well be kill or be killed.' This did nothing to calm Chris's nerves; he explained that he had every faith in the local constabulary, and that being the case he would rather not use a weapon. 'Very well. Be a fool, boy,' the Sergeant snapped, as he put the gun back in a drawer. 'It's your life.' Dr Mayfield placed a caring arm around Chris's shoulder; he knew what he was going through.

The four men carefully went over and over their plans to ensnare their man and rescue the girl. Time passed by, and the Doctor said that Chris needed a rest in order to be ready for the evening. The two men headed for home, leaving Franklin and Thomas, to go through the last of the plans.

Chapter Twenty-Four

The weather was starting to turn bad again; it reminded Chris of the last night that he had seen Jane, that fateful night when he had gone to look for her out on the Fens.

It was shortly after eight, and Chris decided that it was time to go. He tenderly held Emily in his arms and lovingly kissed her, assuring her that everything would be all right.

Dr Mayfield shook Chris's hand, and murmured, 'We are all here waiting for you Christopher, God bless you.' Chris was by now getting quite emotional, especially as Maud wished him well. Kind thoughts and even kinder words, from such a stubborn, stern old spinster, was all too much for him to take.

'Be careful, my darling. I love you; please come home safe,' were the last words offered to Chris by Emily. He held her tight, gently squeezed her, kissed her tenderly on the lips, and then made his way into the night.

He hadn't dressed in too heavy clothing, as he thought that if he needed to run it could thwart his attempts, so he wore only a shirt and a jacket – an old one he had borrowed from Albert, because he did not want to stand out.

As the rain beat fiercely down on his face, he tried to raise the collar of his jacket to gain a little more warmth. Taking a brolly had not been an option; it would be just another item in the way.

Looking up, he could see two shadowy figures in the night. A closer look told him that, indeed, they were Ed and Charlie. As he got nearer the men a feeling of relief struck him as he saw the small frame of Lilly. *Thank God*, he thought, at least she was alive and well.

'Are you ready, Chris?' Ed asked, as he reached the pair. Chris nodded his reply and bent down to see if Lilly was all right. She looked subdued and apprehensive, but the sweet smile that she gave him warmed his heart. 'Look after the girl and follow us,' Ed ordered Chris, 'and don't let her out of your sight.'

Ed looked very serious; this was his business, and he meant every word. In fact, he had such a look of evil determination about him that Chris was only too pleased to obey the man.

He kept a few paces behind Ed and Charlie, holding tight on to Lilly's hand. This gave Chris the perfect opportunity to assure Lilly that all would be OK.

'I'm not a bad man, Lilly,' Chris whispered to her. 'I promise that you will be safe and no harm will come to you; that much I swear.' He squeezed her hand reassuringly.

Lilly looked up at him, and putting her forefinger to her lips whispered, 'Our little secret.' Chris felt even more determined to see this job through, and make sure that Lilly and Emily, and indeed Dr Mayfield, would be safe.

As the house came in sight Ed turned and stopped, handing out the weapons to Charlie and to Chris that he had in one of the sacks. Chris took the gun off Ed and tucked it down the inside of his trousers. A worried look was painted all over the face of Lilly, but a gentle squeeze of her hand comforted her, albeit temporarily.

'Follow me,' Ed ordered, 'and no noise.' He looked down to Lilly. 'You know what you have to do, girl,' Lilly's big brown eyes gazed up in the direction of Ed as she nodded her answer.

They quietly and deliberately approached the Doctor's house; Chris looked around but could see no one. They were in fact twenty minutes early; Chris had anticipated a little more time for the briefing. He could only hope now that Sergeant Thomas would have his men already in place. They approached the entry to the rear of the house, and still no sign of anybody. His heart was now pounding; his breathing was so heavy, that he could feel his body start to tremble.

Ed carefully got out a metal crowbar, and as quietly as he could he forced open the window to the scullery. He turned to Chris, who was now breathing uncontrollably loud, and pointed to his lips in a gesture to tell him to quiet down. Charlie turned also, wearing a look of pure evil across his hardened face.

'Come 'ere, girl,' Ed ordered to Lilly; she slowly edged toward him. He hoisted her up to shoulder height and guided her through the window. Once her little body was inside, he turned her round so her head was now facing him. 'Go to the front door,' he told her. 'You know how many bolts there are on there, we've been through it already.'

Her head slowly lowered, until it was out of sight. She was hanging on the window ledge by her fingertips, until they too disappeared out of sight as she dropped to the floor inside of the house.

Ed prodded Charlie and Chris rather violently, motioning them to the front door. Chris was deep in panic now, anxiously waiting for help to arrive. He knew deep down that the fact that they were early meant that he had to go along with the game until help arrived.

Ed waited impatiently by the front door for little Lilly to unlock it and then open it. A click, followed by a dull clunk, and then the turning of a key. The door slowly opened and Ed barged his way in ahead of the rest.

'Hold her,' he shouted hoarsely to Chris; he could see that he was ushering Lilly to safety, and he had no intention of letting her go. She, along with his sister Emily, would provide their bargaining power if they were compromised and needed hostages.

'The silver, Chris; where's the damn silver?' Ed whispered. Chris pointed to the silver on the table, in the corner of the room, and then pointed to the other rooms; all this was done on purpose to slow them down. Ed was by now starting to get agitated. 'The money,' he demanded, 'where's the money?' Again Chris said nothing, instead he only pointed. He could feel his heart beating louder, thumping at a rapid rate against the walls of his chest.

At that point Ed pointed his gun straight at the head of Chris. Lilly screamed out loud and ran over to her saviour. What followed all seemed to be in slow motion. A loud bang on the front door preceded the entrance of Sergeant Thomas, Constable Franklin and the rest of the police force. Ed stood motionless for a moment, his body frozen as he tried to anticipate their next move; he knew he could not run out the front door, and his hesitation seemed to last an eternity as he made up his mind. In reality it was a matter of seconds as he grabbed hold of Lilly and ran upstairs towards the bedrooms.

Chapter Twenty-Five

Constable Franklin pointed his gun to fire at Ed as he climbed the stairs, dragging Lilly behind him.

'No, for God's sake, man!' Chris screamed 'You could hit the girl.' Franklin's momentum, was interrupted and he lowered his aim, as Chris hurried upstairs after Ed. Charlie was right by Chris's side, safe in the knowledge that they would not fire at him in case they hit Chris; he had by now worked out that Chris was on the side of the police, and he was eager to race up the stairs before him in order to inform Ed. As they reached them Charlie pointed his gun right at the temple of Chris's head. That was his insurance, and his ticket out of there; he had one hand on the gun and the other on Chris's shoulder as they worked their way along the landing corridor. A loud bang startled them both as Ed swung open the door to Emily's room; the bedroom door smashed against the wall and swung back towards them. Ed put his foot in the way and emerged holding his gun, pointing it towards both Emily and Lilly. Chris's heart sank; he knew that he had been rumbled. Ed could see by the look on Charlie's face, and the fact that he was still pointing his gun at the head of Chris, that Chris was a traitor to them. The police had slowly edged their way to the top of the stairs, only to be greeted by the demands of Ed.

'We both walk out of here, right now,' he demanded, 'or three people die; it's your choice.'

Sergeant Thomas screamed abuse at Ed and thumped his fist hard on the banister.

'Let them out,' Dr Mayfield begged, 'but please, take me instead of Chris, Emily and the child.'

'No sir,' Ed replied in a flash, 'they are coming with us.'

Constable Franklin held his arm out, holding back the other officers so that Ed and Charlie could walk down the stairs to the front door along with their hostages. Dr Mayfield tried one last attempt to free them.

'Please, Mr Todd,' he begged once more, 'I will give you whatever you demand as a monetary award, and you have my word as a gentleman that I will not allow the police to follow you.'

This did gain the attention of the two villains, especially Charlie, who was looking more agitated by the minute. Ed pondered for a moment, then shouted, 'No,' and made his way to the front door dragging his hostages with him.

'I will catch you, Todd!' Sergeant Thomas screamed. 'And kill you.' Ed turned and smirked in the direction of the raging Sergeant, then calmly walked out the door followed by Charlie, still menacingly pointing the gun at Chris.

Ed jogged towards the Fens, shouting at the others to keep up. Charlie turned and looked back. Just as the police, headed by the irate Sergeant Thomas, were leaving the house he hoisted up his gun, outstretched his arm and fired in the direction of the ensuing pack.

This gave the men a precious few seconds to gain more ground. Poor Emily only had a dress on; she had had no time to grab a coat. The cold January rain drove down relentlessly on them as they walked on the Fens.

They had now gained enough of a lead over their pursuers to chastise Chris. Ed calmly walked toward him, and with a well-timed right hook to the jaw sent him sprawling to the ground. Chris tried to get up to defend himself, but the gun that Charlie had trained on him forced him to stay put while Ed relentlessly kicked him repeatedly in the head and body, all the time screaming at him that he was a traitor. Blood poured from the helpless man's wounds, as Ed just did not seem to tire.

'Please, Ed, please!' Emily screamed at her brother. 'I love him. We are to be married, please don't hurt him.' With that she threw herself on top of Chris to protect her lover. Ed stopped momentarily; he tried to compose himself and come to terms with what he had just heard.

Charlie crouched over Chris and screamed, 'Shall I kill him boss? Shall I finish him?'

'Not yet, Charlie,' Ed replied. 'We will finish him, but we will get away first.' With that they dragged Chris to his feet and forced him to walk on. He was beaten quite badly but managed to stagger along.

The night was getting colder, and the rain was now turning to sleet and snow as the two parties headed deeper into the Fens. Sergeant Thomas was out of control as he ordered his men to catch up and find the villains. They spread themselves out in a line and strained their eyes, as visibility was getting worse, to find the fugitives. Emily was shivering uncontrollably; Chris removed his coat and placed it over her shoulders, telling her to share it with Lilly. Ed and Charlie seemed oblivious to the cold as they hurried on, demanding that the hostages do the same. Ed grabbed Emily by her hair; pulling her beautiful face to one side, he pressed his face right into hers and screamed, 'You cannot, you will not marry the traitor, because I am going to kill him any moment now.'

Emily, although in some discomfort, looked her brother in the eyes and said, 'No, Ed, you will have to kill me first.' Ed never let go of her hair as he pulled her even closer toward him. The anger was set deep in his eyes; she had witnessed that look of rage many times before.

'You will not marry him, and I'll tell you for why, sister of mine,' he screamed, still holding tight to her hair. 'Because you cannot marry a dead man.' He pulled her so hard that she fell into the mud. This angered Chris, and he went straight for Ed. The sharp prod of gun metal in the back of his head stopped him dead in his tracks. Charlie had his weapon pointed right at the back of his head. 'I swear, Ed,' Chris stuttered, still very much in pain from his beating. 'You harm Emily and I will kill you.'

Ed smirked in anger and turned his gun to Chris; he slowly walked toward, him never lowering his aim.

'God no, please,' Emily whispered as he got nearer to him. 'Please, please no, don't kill him,' Lilly cried, tears rolling down her pretty little cheeks. They both could only sit and helplessly watch, as Ed got right up to within a foot of Chris's head. He pointed his gun, and a loud bang echoed all over the Fens.

Chapter Twenty-Six

Lilly buried her head into her hands; Emily was just frozen to the spot speechless, and unable to move. The heavy sound of a body hitting the rain-sodden ground was too much for Emily to take; she screamed, and too scared to even look, buried her head down into the mud and cried uncontrollably.

Ed was panicking, shouting out over and over again, 'How? How?' Emily raised her head to see that it was Charlie lying motionless on the ground; Chris was still standing, only just, but alive nevertheless.

Ed ordered Emily to her feet and used her as a human shield as the police advanced on him. The well-aimed shot by the ever-calm Constable Franklin had once again saved the life of Chris.

'Give yourself up, Ed Todd,' Sergeant Thomas bawled. 'While you are still alive and able to do so, or you will join your friend.'

Ed was now on his own with three hostages to encumber him. But visibility in the falling snow was very poor, and it was not long before Ed had once more gained a few precious yards on the police. He could hear them in the distance, advancing on him, but surrender was not an option; he knew that prison beckoned, even hanging if he killed one of his hostages, and that was if they didn't kill him first.

Chris saw for the first time fear in Ed's eyes; he had three hostages and was busy pointing his gun in three different directions. Trying to compose himself and think things through, Chris made a snap decision; he deliberately pushed Emily to the ground. This distracted the attention of Ed, as he looked to see what had happened, Chris made a move and threw his aching body at the villain. The gun fell to the ground as Chris dived on top of Ed; the two men wrestled in the mud while Chris screamed at Emily and Lilly to run. They stood still for a moment, hesitating, not wanting to leave him there. Emily moved to help Chris in his struggle, but again he screamed with what little energy he had left for her to run. 'For God's sake, run, and take the child with you!' he begged. Emily, though heartbroken at having to make a decision, decided that it was the right thing to do – if not for her sake, then for little Lilly's. She grabbed hold of the girl and ran, dragging Lilly behind her toward safety.

Chris managed to pull away from Ed and staggered to his feet; while Ed fumbled in the dark for his gun, Chris remembered that he too had a gun tucked down his trousers. As Ed rose to his feet he pointed the gun at him and told him to give himself up.

Ed just sneered at him and slowly advanced toward Chris. 'Did you really think that I would give you a loaded gun?'

Chris's heart sank; he did not even bother to pull the trigger, as he knew deep down that the gun was not loaded.

He saw the punch coming toward him, and tried hard to avoid it so he had a chance of defending himself, but his cold tired and battered body failed to react in time.

The impact took Chris straight off his feet, and once again he was on the ground as Ed rained even more blows to his already battered body and head.

He could hear in the distance the police calling Emily and Lilly toward them; he knew they were safe. It was only him and Ed now and he did not fancy his chances, but in the back of his mind, just knowing they were safe was a consolation.

It was now biting cold out on the Fens; he lay face down in the mud as the heavy falling snow formed a blanket over his aching, wounded body. He started to drift off into an almost unconscious oblivion.

Reality dawned when Ed dragged him back to his feet. 'You are coming with me, boy,' Ed ordered. A dazed and almost incoherent Chris did as he was ordered and staggered to his feet. It was becoming harder to walk now, the snow was getting heavier and was lying deep on the ground. It was becoming harder for them to walk away and easier for the police to follow their trail, they just had to follow the footsteps.

'You will never live to see my sister again, let alone marry her,' Ed tormented Chris, while forcing him along. Chris, however, was in a bad way; he had had two ferocious beatings, and the cold was now draining his body. He had given his coat to Emily, so that all he was wearing now was a shirt. He could feel himself drifting in and out of consciousness.

'Keep up,' Ed shouted, as Chris slowed more and more. He stared into the void; he strained his eyes to focus, but the snow just kept coming down, blurring his vision.

Every step felt like an immense effort; his legs felt heavy, and he could feel his heart slowing down. His mind was becoming confused; he knew he was running out of time.

Nothing Ed could do to him could worsen what was actually happening. In a moment of sheer defiance, Chris stood still and declared that he was not moving another inch; in reality, he knew that he could not anyway. He knew that if he carried on walking then he would surely die, and even if he didn't die at the mercy of the weather, then he would die at the hands of the villainous Ed.

Ed screamed at Chris, 'Keep moving or I will kill you!' Chris was unable to move another step even if he wanted to, and he didn't; he just did not have the strength or the impetus.

'No,' he replied defiantly: 'I'm not taking one more step.'

Ed snarled at Chris; he was himself now starting to feel the effects of the weather. To him Chris was nothing more now than a burden; Ed turned and headed toward him for the last time.

Chris could do nothing but stand and stare as Ed approached him face on. He turned the gun around, and with the handle he clubbed Chris ferociously around the head; a second attempt to do the same was thwarted by the collapse of the weakened, badly beaten man.

Chris crumpled to the ground; he could draw on no more energy to help him survive. Ed pointed the gun at him mercilessly; Chris tried desperately to open his eyes, but his body had given in to the tiredness that was all too familiar with hypothermia.

'Give yourself up, Edward Todd!' reverberated around the ice-cold Fens. He was indeed surrounded by police; he aimed one last kick to the head of Chris, and then pointed his gun in the direction of where he had heard the voices.

Ed fired two shots into the night, then decided to run. A further three shots rang out, and Ed fell to the ground. Sergeant Thomas stood over his victim, and fired one last shot into his chest.

'Nobody saw that one,' he shouted, as he stood over the body of Edward Todd; a few gurgling noises was all that he could muster as his life drained away from him.

'Find Christopher,' Sergeant Thomas ordered, as they frantically searched the area for the man.

Emily and Lilly helped in the search; they knew that he was nearby, but visibility was so bad that it was making the search almost impossible.

'Over here!' came the cry from nearby; a lantern was held over the spot so they all could gather round. 'Make way,' Dr Mayfield ordered as he headed toward the place where Chris lay.

His lifeless body lay still as the newly fallen snow that formed a white shroud over him. Emily screamed out, 'Oh no! Please, God no,' as Dr Mayfield frantically tried to find a pulse.

He looked up to Emily and shook his head, taking off his own coat to place over the body. 'Please don't go, Chris,' Emily cried. 'I love you, please don't give in, please don't leave me.'

Constable Franklin pulled Emily back; he watched Dr Mayfield try desperately to revive Chris. Lilly stood next to Emily. She was now wearing Chris's coat and crying uncontrollably, hoping and praying that he would be OK.

Emily wanted to say so much more but was overcome with a dreadful feeling of grief. She stared down, sobbing, at the lifeless body of the man that she loved.

Chapter Twenty-Seven

'I love you, Chris, please don't give in, please don't leave me.' Those words replayed over and over in his semi-conscious mind. A flicker in his eyelids, and a slight movement of his hand showed those that were gathered around that there was life in his body. The muffled noises that formed a hazy background were now sounding more like words, as he slowly drifted back into consciousness. He did not feel cold any more, he felt more comfortable, and warm, and could sense a great deal of love around him; he could feel his hand being squeezed as he slowly opened his eyes.

'Chris, do you know where you are?' a voice whispered. He was awake, but not yet fully coherent; at this moment in time all of the voices seemed to merge into one. Then one voice stood out. 'Chris, my love, it is me Jane. Can you hear me? Please answer me, or make a sign.'

With that his eyes opened wide. 'Jane...' he whispered, 'Jane, where am I? Where is Emily?'

'Oh, Chris, you came back to me,' Jane sobbed. 'I always knew you would come back to me.'

She leaned over and gently kissed him on the lips. The hazy figures standing over his bed were all coming into focus. His parents were there, Jane's parents were there, and Jane's younger sister Chloe was there too. Chris was now starting to familiarise himself with his new surroundings. He looked over at Chloe and saw that she was the exact double of little Lilly the matchstick girl, only less emaciated. He looked long at his own parents, and then Jane's, for any other connection; could they have been Maud, or Albert, or one of them Dr Mayfield? But there were no resemblances there.

Over the following couple of hours, Chris learned that he had come down with hypothermia out on the Fens. He had fallen and hit his head, which in turn had caused the swelling on the brain, and to add to all of that pneumonia had set in to his tired, frail body. To all around him, and even many of the doctors and nurses that had cared for him, it was indeed a miracle that he was alive.

The families left Chris and Jane to spend some time together. Although he was still frail and weak, he felt that he had to share his experience with Jane. After all, she had asked him when the family had left, who Emily was.'

Chris went through the whole story, doing his best to leave out the intimate details. Jane listened patiently. Although she tried to tell him that it was only a dream, his precision on times and dates, and the details of the era which he claimed to have visited did make her think.

'Look, Chris,' she pointed out, holding a mirror close to his face. 'You have no bruises, my love; you were in no fight, only your fight for life, and you were not hit in the face by a gun handle.'

Chris was totally amazed. 'But it all seemed so real, Jane,' he explained. 'I was there, you were Emily, Chloe was Lilly... don't you see?'

'Yes, Chris, exactly,' Jane jumped in. 'Can't you see, my love, that all of those people in your dreams were characters that your mind contrived? They were all people that you know and love, only in your dream you placed them in different situations; you used their faces as a comfort to you.'

He smiled at Jane, and squeezed tight on her hand. 'And the church?' he asked. 'Saint Peter's in Hanly village? For God's sake, Jane, neither of us have ever visited Hanly village.'

'Not that you can remember, my love,' Jane replied. 'You may have done years ago, and just stored the information in your subconscious.'

It all seemed so surreal to Chris. Just then the Doctor walked in. 'Good to have you back, Christopher,' he said in his Asian accent.

Jane looked at Chris and smiled. He knew what that smile meant: indeed this doctor was not Mayfield and that was for sure; wrong colour, certainly a different shape, and far better looking. *Doctor...* Chris thought this man looked more like a film star.

'You must try to sleep, Christopher,' the Doctor ordered. 'You have been through a great deal; your body needs rest if we are to let you go home soon.'

'Will you stay please, Jane?' Chris asked.

'Of course I will, my love,' Jane sweetly replied. She placed her hand on his forehead, and he lay down and within seconds drifted off into a peaceful slumber.

What seemed like a moment later, but was in fact a good couple of hours, he woke to find Jane still there, with her head on his chest, herself fast asleep.

He gently shook her, and told her that she should go home and rest. He felt selfish asking her to stay, 'Please,' Chris begged her, 'you need a good night's sleep; I'm OK now, and I think that I'll sleep the night through.' Jane reluctantly agreed; she had missed out on so much sleep that she was only too glad to leave him, now that she knew he was safe.

They kissed goodnight, and Jane left for home. Chris laid down his head and once more fell into a deep sleep.

The rattling of a hospital trolley and the clatter of cups and saucers woke Chris from his slumber.

'Good morning,' a pleasant voice spoke. 'Would you like tea or coffee?' Chris stared into the middle-aged lady's eyes, hoping to recognise her from the time which he had left behind, but nothing, her face wasn't familiar.

'Tea, please,' he answered, feeling a little disappointed that she was not a face that he knew. How could this be, he thought, how could he have invented all of those people?

Here he was alive and well, back in January 2008, and yet he could not stop thinking of Emily, Lilly and Dr Mayfield. What had happened to them, were they safe? Did he die in 1898?

Stop it, he thought. Jane must be right; he had slept the night through and not dreamt about any of them. If it had all been a dream, then it was an explicit one.

He had no bruises, no cuts; the clothes in his locker were his jeans and the jumper that he was found in. No visible facts could back up his claim to have lived, albeit temporarily, in 1898, so the only possible conclusion was that it was a dream.

A portly gentleman entered the room. 'How are you feeling today, Christopher?'

Chris looked up at the man. 'Good God, Dr Mayfield!' he shouted out.

'Yes, that's correct, but how did you know that?' the Doctor replied curiously.

'You wouldn't believe me if I told you,' Chris answered despondently.

Chapter Twenty-Eight

The Doctor was pleased with Chris's recovery, and Chris didn't bother explaining to him how he recognised him. The few minutes' conversation that he had with the Doctor convinced him that he must have heard his name while in his coma, and subconsciously added him to his dream.

It was a very grateful, although somewhat disillusioned, Christopher that left the hospital two days later to rebuild his life.

Walking back into his apartment felt very strange; once again he was surrounded by all of the luxuries that were a part of everyday life in 2008.

Jane could see that he was still perturbed by what he had dreamt. He would not let it lie, and the more that he told her the more she thought it all very strange to say the least. She suggested that they go and visit the village of Hanly. 'I will drive you,' she suggested, 'it is far too long a walk to go over the Fens.'

A wonderful warm feeling overcame Chris, as they parked their car in Hanly. Holding tight on to Jane's hand, they walked up and down the high street. Although only several miles from where they both lived, Chris had never visited Hanly before; not in this life anyway.

He walked along, pointing out landmarks with great accuracy to Jane; some buildings had obviously gone, but others he pointed out before they even got to them.

The Doctor's house was still standing, although the police station had long since been demolished. It still looked a splendid, grand old house. Chris convinced Jane to go with him as he approached and knocked on the door. He had no idea as to what to expect, but sheer shock and disbelief hit him as the door opened. It was Dr Mayfield. Both men looked shocked; Chris fumbled out some kind of explanation and the Doctor smiled at Chris and invited the couple in.

Chris went through the entire story; he even took the Doctor and Jane on a guided tour around the house. 'Well,' he exclaimed, 'explain that away as a dream if you dare!'

'It was no dream, Christopher,' Dr Mayfield informed him. He told Chris and Jane that he was Dr Paul Mayfield, third generation of Mayfields, all doctors to follow in the steps of the innovative Doctor Edmund Mayfield.

His grandfather used to tell him stories of his father Edmund Mayfield, and of his great friend Christopher Price, who became a local hero after saving his true love Emily, and the little matchstick girl Lilly. Dr Edmund Mayfield married in the summer of 1898, and his wife gave birth to Peter Mayfield in the spring of 1900.

He went on to tell them that Christopher and Emily married on the Saturday as arranged, and Lilly became their maid, right up until the day she got married herself.

Christopher and Emily had four children, two boys and two girls, all of whom got married and had children of their own. Christopher died at the age of eighty in 1950, Emily died the following year aged seventy-three, and they were both buried in Saint Peter's churchyard.

'I will take you over there,' he suggested.

'Oh, yes please,' Chris replied. A short walk over to the church brought back more memories to Chris. A cold shiver ran down the whole of his body as he stood at the grave that held the two bodies.

Throughout all of this Jane lovingly held his hand; she too felt a cold shiver. After all, according to Chris there lay their remains, in a previous life.

A huge monument stood where Doctor Edmund Mayfield lay at rest. A little further down was the grave of Lilly Brown; her life has been cut short by the great influenza epidemic, and she passed on at just forty.

Back at the Doctor's house, he explained that as soon as he had seen Chris, and recognised him, it had brought a certain clarity to a story that had been passed down through the generations of the Mayfield family.

'Why do I remember nothing else?' Chris asked. 'Why does my memory stop on the Fens?'

'Have you ever heard of regression, Chris?' the Doctor asked.

'Yes,' Chris replied, 'Your great-grandfather virtually pioneered the concept, and I was one of his first successes.'

'So it was true then,' Dr Mayfield exclaimed, overcome with joy.

He looked at Chris, and said, 'The only explanation that I can give you is that during your coma, your mind went into regression; you did not physically go there, but you went back to a previous life, a life that existed for you, and indeed Jane, one hundred and ten years ago.

'Hypnosis may help you retrace the events that preceded, or even happened after your experience in the Fens. But if you want my advice, I would leave it there.'

'But why?' Chris asked. 'Why just that bit of my past life?'

The Doctor explained that what he had experienced was what was happening at the exact date and time all those years ago, while he lay in his coma.

'It was a freak of nature,' he explained. 'For a short time your mind, even your soul, travelled back to enjoy a previous life.' He went on to add, 'We have but one soul, Christopher, but many vehicles in which that soul will reside until it finally rests. What you had was a wonderful experience, a brief glimpse back to a body that your soul was once so happy to live in; your soul temporarily got mixed up between two lives.'

Chris looked at Jane; they both felt overwhelmed at what they had seen and heard. He decided there and then to leave the past where it was; that was then and now he intended to love and cherish Jane.

As usual many thoughts crossed his mind; were he and Jane actually living a regression, now, a hundred years in the future? A smile beamed across his handsome face. 'All too complicated, is this,' he laughed.

'Well, Christopher, it has been an honour, and a dream, no: a story that became a reality,' the Doctor said, shaking his hand warmly.

'Goodbye, my good friend,' Dr Mayfield said as Chris and Jane left the house. Chris looked back in astonishment; could the Doctor actually be his old friend, himself reincarnated?

'Until the next time!' Christopher shouted back; he glanced back and could see his friend returning the smile.

'Indeed, my good friend...' he shouted back, 'until the next time!'

Chris and Jane walked hand in hand to their car. 'Come on, Jane,' Chris said smiling with joy. 'This is the start of the rest of our lives.'

'And beyond!' Jane replied.

'Well, here's to the beyond then,' Chris smiled, as they hugged and tenderly kissed. 'Here is to us.'

Printed in the United Kingdom by
Lightning Source UK Ltd., Milton Keynes
142416UK00001B/38/P